Fire in the Woods

I took off running, heading in the direction of the smoke—the direction of my morning run. The direction of the cabin. This was less likely a forest fire than it was that old cabin burning, and the intensifying smell of gasoline suggested arson.

It was then that I remembered the glimpse of movement at the cabin's window that morning, and my chest contracted with dread. I wished I'd stopped to grab my gun, which I keep stowed under a stack of towels on the shelf alongside my mattress.

The dread turned to cold fear when I broke into the cabin's clearing to see—not the ruins afire as I'd expected, but the cabin's ancient boards converted to a funeral pyre on which a body was burning.

He's come here! was my sole thought before pain splintered through my head and the curtain fell.

A Molly Piper Mystery

Falling from Grace

Patricia Brooks

A Dell Book

Published by
Dell Publishing
a division of
Bantam Doubleday Dell Publishing Group, Inc.
1540 Broadway
New York, New York 10036

This novel is a work of fiction. Names, characters, places, and incidents either are the product of the author's imagination or are used fictitiously. Any resemblance to actual persons, living or dead, events, or locales is entirely coincidental.

If you purchased this book without a cover you should be aware that this book is stolen property. It was reported as "unsold and destroyed" to the publisher and neither the author nor the publisher has received any payment for this "stripped book."

Copyright © 1998 by Patricia Brooks

All rights reserved. No part of this book may be reproduced or transmitted in any form or by any means, electronic or mechanical, including photocopying, recording, or by any information storage and retrieval system, without the written permission of the Publisher, except where permitted by law.

The trademark Dell® is registered in the U.S. Patent and Trademark Office.

ISBN: 0-440-22607-4

Printed in the United States of America

Published simultaneously in Canada

December 1998

10 9 8 7 6 5 4 3 2 1

WCD

*To my mother,
the original mystery writer in the family,
who is probably co-plotting this series
from the other side.*

My thanks to the cottages at Hedgebrook Women Writers' Residence for their faith in Molly's first novel, the three blissful months spent there, and for introducing me to the island that is the *fictionalized* model for Prince Island, now my permanent home.

My continued thanks to my agent, Carol McCleary of the Wilshire Agency in Beverly Hills; to my editor, Jacquie Miller; and to Kathy Lord, the copy editor on this book, for her meticulous care and mathematical skills.

CHAPTER 1

I WAITED FOR THE LOOK. Maybe you know the one, that startled stare of disbelief that says, "*You?!* You can't be."

In my case, the *can't-be* is a private detective, and the disbelief stems from my gender (female), my age (twenty-six), and last but never least, my size (four feet nine inches; ninety-seven pounds).

If you have trouble visualizing those stats, picture your basic female Olympic gymnast, that sturdy, eternally pubescent body type honed by years of triple-flipping across the floor, dancing on a skinny balance beam, vaulting over massive barriers, and swinging over and under those slippery uneven bars several times your height. Such skills weren't included in the certification test I took for P.I. legitimacy in Washington State, but already they've come in handy. Maybe more so than my year as a Chicago cop.

But this woman standing in my office doorway didn't have that look. In fact, her gaze alighted on me only for a moment before it took off, darting about the room like a small bird desperate to find a window.

"Ms. Abbott?" I said. "Come in, please. Have a seat." I gestured toward the client chair, a shabby but comfortable gray plush monster I found left on a curb with the garbage. It's soft and deep, easier to get into than out of. Which I thought couldn't hurt business either.

When she didn't move, I leaned back in my swivel chair behind the desk to await her decision. She had called from the Prince Island Women's Center, just four blocks from my office in the little town of Grace, and the source of most of my business. She was still holding my card, in fact, in the same hand with which she gripped the strap of the bag over her right shoulder. The long fingers of her other hand were nervously shredding a corner of the card until, abruptly, she moved to a chair and sat.

It was not the comfy chair she chose, however, but one of the two metal folding chairs to the left of the desk, meant to accommodate any others in the client party. Already, my knowledge of pop psychology was assigning her low points for self-esteem.

She set the big beige purse on her lap and wrapped her arms about it. The bag was one of those huge vinyl numbers advertised in catalogs as having compartments for everything you could possibly need, and Mary Alice Abbott looked to be a woman in need.

She was not unattractive—at least potentially—tall and slim, probably only five or six years older than my twenty-six years. But she had the shadow of middle age upon her, a slump to the mouth and shoulders that suggested a lifetime of disappointment. Her thin hair was coiled on her head in a style several generations out of date, her clothes equally unfashionable—straight gray wool skirt reaching midcalf above sensible shoes, starched white blouse downplaying ample breasts. Her complexion was flawless but pale, as though she'd been ill. Even her eyes, a vivid cobalt blue, had an abstracted quality, as if she'd left some vital part of herself behind.

Altogether, the woman struck me as a person whose connection to life was tenuous, like an orchid that would wither outside a greenhouse. And whatever had brought her to me had put enough of a scare in her to force her out of that shelter.

Her eyes focused on mine at last and she spoke. "It's about my sister," she said. "I have to find her."

I suppressed an impulse to sigh. When would a case for more than missing persons ever walk through that door? In the eight months since I'd set up shop on this island, I'd found two runaway daughters, three errant husbands, and a birth mother. Not that I didn't appreciate the business—any business that came my way in those first months—but how could a P.I. earn any real rep without something juicy to work on?

Professionalism, professionalism. I sat up straighter and directed my attention back to the client. "Has she been missing long?"

She looked at me, her thin brows creasing over her nose. "I'm not sure," she said slowly. "We haven't . . . been in touch that long."

I struggled to make sense of the statement. "It's been a while, then, since you've seen each other?"

"Oh, I haven't seen her."

"Haven't seen her?" I echoed foolishly.

"She only just contacted me, two weeks ago now. But we were to meet and she never came. I haven't heard from her since."

She opened the purse then and took out a packet of three letters bound by a frayed blue ribbon. Her hand seemed to contemplate extending them to me but instead pulled the packet back against her breast. "You understand, my mother must never know of this," she said, her intense eyes staring into mine. "At least not yet."

I murmured something about confidentiality, withdrawing the hand I'd offered to receive the letters.

She went on, her voice hoarse, as though she didn't use it much. "My mother has given me everything; I don't want her hurt."

I felt at a bit of a loss to know what to ask next; I hadn't fully processed what I'd already heard. "Have you known you had a sister? Before she contacted you, that is?"

She hesitated. "Sometimes I seem to have memories of her. But my mother said Alice was only my invisible friend. All children have them, you know, so I guess I just believed that."

"Alice?" I said. The woman had identified herself over the phone as Mary Alice Abbott. I felt an involuntary thrill of excitement as the words *evil twin* flashed, unbidden, through my brain. "Was—is she your twin?" I asked.

"Oh, no. She's older. My big sister. She says I was still little when she got sent away. So I could have been imagining, like Mother said."

"But you weren't."

"No."

"And you're sure the person you're hearing from now is legitimate?"

"Oh, yes. Yes, I knew it immediately."

She seemed to pass into a reverie again, her eyes losing focus, her hands moving across the letters like a child caressing its blanky.

"What do you remember particularly about her?" I asked, to jog her back.

"She protected me," she answered promptly. "I remember that she protected me."

"From . . . ?"

Her face blanked out again. After a considerable pause I ventured, "From your parents maybe?"

The vivid eyes refocused. "Oh, no, my mother has always protected me. My uncle too, Mother's brother. Maybe too much, you could say."

"And your father?"

"That's just it," she said. "Apparently, it's memories Alice has been having about him that have led her to contact me. She started going to a group because she couldn't sleep. They told her she was having 'post-traumatic stress.' I looked it up: memories of abuse."

"Sexual abuse?"

"I guess," she said faintly.

"Did you experience any such abuse yourself?"

Her eyes widened with alarm. "No! Oh, goodness, no." Then, collecting herself, "I hardly even remember him. Mother says I was almost three when he left us."

"What do you remember about him?"

"Nothing, really. I saw a picture once though. He was very handsome. I think my mother really loved him—you know, that way."

Belatedly, I remembered my new resolve to take notes during first interviews. My memory tends to get lost in impressions and forgets details. I pulled a yellow legal pad and gnawed ballpoint from the desk's top drawer and reviewed the basics, looking up periodically for confirmation. I headed the sheet *Mary Alice Abbott* and asked for her address, home and work phone numbers, social-security number, and birth date. She was, it turned out, also twenty-seven—twenty-eight come next August.

"Your sister contacted you two weeks ago."

"Yes. The sixth of March."

"By letter."

"Yes."

"But you have not actually met her in person."

"No. She finally wrote that she wanted to, last week, but then she didn't come. Or maybe she thought I didn't. She said ten in the morning, but I only got the letter at four that afternoon. The mail usually comes early at work, but that day there was a substitute and it came late. So I went right there, to the restaurant, but I didn't see anyone who could be her. I've been back every day since, at lunchtime, and after work until my mother started suspecting something. But Alice never came. At least she never introduced herself. But I'm sure I'd know her if I saw her."

"What was the restaurant?"

"The Queen's . . ."

"Queen's Rest? Above Port Angel?"

"Yes. I was glad it wasn't the house she picked to meet at. I mean, she's angry at Mother, says she sent her away. I'm kind of worried about it, to tell you the truth."

"You think she might harm your mother?"

Fear stiffened her features. "Oh, I hope not. But who knows what she might be capable of? What anybody might?"

There was something there to be pursued, but I let it go for the moment in the interest of a continuous history.

"So you were how young when she left?"

"I don't know exactly, since I don't really remember, but Alice says I was still little. She says she started running away but kept coming back to check on me, to be sure I was okay. Then Mother sent her away for good."

"Do you know where?"

"No. But it was to some woman. Who always read the Bible."

"Have you any idea who that was?"

"No."

I backtracked a bit. "You say 'the house.' Does that mean you're still living with your mother?"

Mary Alice gave me another of her curious blank looks. "Yes," she said, the look adding, "of course."

"And the name. You say your sister was named Alice, but your name is Mary Alice?"

She came up with a small smile, which seemed to give her face a needed rest. "I guess Mother started calling me Mary Alice after Alice left. Maybe so I wouldn't wonder why she wasn't there." The smile disappeared. "I haven't asked Mother about any of this though. I'm afraid to. That's why I've come to you, to find out."

CHAPTER 2

THE QUESTIONS AND ANSWERS CONTINUED for a while but without much more in the way of hard information. Mary Alice's address put her in Serenity Shores, an area of old-money homes tucked behind a bluff on the eastern edge of Grace. She wasn't sucking the proverbial silver spoon, however; she worked eight to five at the Redi-Clean dry cleaners, up Highway #309 from where the ferry lands in Port Angelina.

I didn't have to ask why she'd chosen me; she volunteered that she didn't have much money, and mine are the lowest rates around. "My mother does," she said, "from her parents. They died, in some accident, a long time ago. But this is something I'm doing, and I don't want her to know."

She was right about the rates: first hour consult free, then $20 an hour plus expenses. As opposed to $30–$100 an hour for those with more experience. Or more gall. I'd printed the rates right on my card, hoping for just this sort of cash-short clientele. Until, of course, my overwhelming success would begin to attract those with deeper pockets. Then I could do these for free.

I considered that initial session a success when

Mary Alice Abbott signed a contract and did not hesitate to write a check for the $500 advance. She asked only that I hold the check a day so she could transfer the funds from her savings account. A more significant vote of confidence was that she left her packet of letters with me, to peruse before our scheduled meeting the next day.

I left the office soon after. It was nearly five o'clock and I was eager to get away for a good uninterrupted read. I'm not one of these people who can sit by a trilling phone until the machine answers. That must take a level of cool I have yet to achieve. Or am even going for.

Outside, the March wind was working hard to maintain its reputation for bluster. Most people were tilted slightly forward to compensate if they were headed upwind. Those of us under a hundred pounds just have to tilt a little further.

I turned right on Sage, then cut through the Nature's Bounty drugstore parking lot to Nutmeg, passing women clutching hats and scarves over their heads to protect their hairdos. That's one problem I don't have. So far as I know, there have been no wirehaired terriers among my ancestors, but you couldn't tell it by my hair. Cocoa brown like my eyes, and thick, it resists all styling and most combs and brushes. So it's carefree by default.

It was still early in the year for tourists, so I headed for The Blue Heron, a café on Chamomile that does nothing to announce itself from the street, but that keeps being discovered by the tourists for its third-floor view of the bay. At high season The Heron would be packed and noisy, which is why most full-time residents of this island favor winter. What discomforts come with the weather are made up for by the peace and quiet that descend when the last BMW has crossed on the ferry, headed back to Seattle.

Me, I'm crazy about the place, and the wilder the weather, the better I like it. Some fifty miles long and half that wide, Prince Island rises out of Puget Sound like it belongs more to the sea than the land. If you've ever seen a dolphin or a killer whale breach water, that's roughly the shape—head tucked, back arched, tail curving beneath it in a graceful arc. An eclectic mix of farm and fancy, there are five towns, four bays, two ports, and a naval base studding the island's periphery like barnacles, its guts occupied by Shepherd's Woods, still holding out against the developer's ax.

The name was originally Pyrus Island, after the Greek ship's captain who ran aground here, thus founding the place. But as the sixties were winding down, those with brains still relatively unfried headed north from Haight-Ashbury, and some ended up here, buying an acre of woods for next to nothing and settling down as peaceful, moderately productive citizens living lightly on the land.

True to their sense of romance, the hippies took to calling it Pirates Island. And though the name never went out on any official letterhead, it was used by practically everybody, to the consternation of the burgeoning respectable element arriving with money to spend and development in mind. After many failed attempts to rename it for one or another of those dignitaries, the powers that came to be—bankers, lawyers, realtors—eventually joined forces, and the name Prince Island carried the day. Some die-hard sixties folk still call it Pirates; and tour guides and barkeeps keep the theme alive; but most of us are resigned to Prince.

I had scarcely made it to my favorite corner table at The Heron before my fingers were wriggling the blue ribbon off the packet of letters and fanning them out before me on the round white top. Already my imagination was charged with the case's hints of simmering grudges and familial betrayals.

The three letters were in identical square blue envelopes, the lightweight kind more likely found in discount stores than in fine stationery shops, the boxed contents visible beneath a plastic lid. The pages I extracted from the first were of the same blue, thin enough to have been billed as suitable for airmail.

The letters were addressed to *Miss Mary Abbott, Redi-Clean Dry Cleaners, 1220 Highway 309, Port Angelina, WA*. The postmarks on all three indicated they had been mailed from Port Angel, as the locals call it, four or five days apart in date. The postmark on the first was March 5, though the date on the first page read March 1. I wondered how long this sister had been on the island, perhaps watching Mary Alice through the cleaner's drive-up window, or secreting herself in the bushes outside the Abbott home. I felt that tingling sensation in my scalp I get when I think about stalkers. It's the helplessness, I guess, not knowing that they're there. No wonder Mary Alice was nervous—and felt protective of her mother, who was the apparent target of Alice's anger.

I smoothed the delicate pages of the first letter carefully on the iron table, wondering whether it had been Mary Alice's or her sister's hands that had clutched them, making the faint smudges at the upper left and lower right corners of the paper—probably the marks of perspiring fingertips; they looked too shallow to have been teardrops.

The handwriting was cramped and slanted to the right, with lots of peaks and sharp descents. It read:

> *I dont know how to start. I been writing this thing a hundred times in my head but it never comes out right. So I guess I just have to say it. I have come back. Do you remember your Big Sister Alice the one you called My Alice? Well Im her and I have come back to you.*
>
> *I don't know what they told you but I didn't just leave you just like that. Even when I was running I kept coming back to be sure you were okay. But then instead of making him stop the jealous bitch sent me away for good to that awful woman to be like her slave.*

From the periphery of my vision, I caught sight of a bright spot of blue and looked up to see The Heron staff apron on the form of a slender woman with bleached-blond hair and eyes as bright as her uniform. She was holding her order pad at the ready, and her fixed stare suggested she'd been standing there awhile. I smiled apologetically and gave her my usual order for chicken salad on wheat and mulled cider, my attention drawn quickly back to the page.

> *I didnt stay there long let me tell you. All that reading the Bible didn't do her much good I could see she was still mean as a witch always telling me how I was damned to hell. Soon as I could I got out of there and been on my own ever since. Unless you count the year and a half I was married to that nogood deadbeat I dont.*
>
> *Why I came is because I started remembering things more than before about him your father. I just got a job a real job and everything my own place then I dont know it seemed like I was imagining things somebody coming up on me in the night in secret doing things I wouldnt even let*

johns do when I was grownup. It got so I couldnt sleep so finly I went to this doctor for sleeping pills but he said I should talk to somebody. I couldnt pay for a shrink or anything so I started going to this group at the rape crisus and they helped me remember and then I started to worry about you back here.

Its so confusing the way it comes. I did some coke and stuff when I was on the street but this is difront. They have a name for it postmatic stress from when you were a kid from sex abuse. So I wondered if you maybe have it too if he started on you after I was gone. You were still little then but maybe later.

I been watching you all grownup. And that bitch of a mother she hasnt changed much. But I dont see him so maybe she kicked him out too high time. I keep trying to come up and say something to you but seems like I cant do it Im to afraid. She said I wasnt good enuf for you then so Im probly still not but I always did my best for you and I really want to be sisters like we were. Maybe I just have to talk to you like this first before Ill be ready. But please think and see if you have any of those kinds of memorys from when you were a kid and Ill try to be with you soon. Just whatever you do dont let her see this letter Im not ready for her yet.

Your Big Sister Alice

A waiter came with my sandwich, and I munched while I read. There was one more letter before the last note urging that they meet. The second was shorter but expressed the same emotions of hope and fear, swaying one way, then the other. I was reminded of studies of approach–avoidance conditioning: here a shock, there a treat, but never knowing which would come next. If this Alice was anything like her sister Mary, she'd been stung to caution.

From the language of the letters I gathered that Alice hadn't had much education, maybe none since she'd begun "running," as the runaways call it. And there were references to living on the street, surviving by selling her body. Judging from Mary Alice's demeanor, I'd have assumed her mother was a stickler for etiquette and had never uttered the word *sex* out loud in her life. Yet this other daughter had apparently been pushed straight into the arms of pimps and dope dealers. This was one mother I was going to have to see for myself.

I downed the last of my cider and headed for home.

CHAPTER 3

ACTUALLY, I HAVE THREE HOMES. Though I guess you could argue I have none, in the more traditional sense.

First there's my office in Grace, a village of less than a thousand souls tucked into the smiling mouth of the dolphin. I'm on the second floor of a semirestored Victorian on Dahlia, between Sage and Sassafras. (The hippies, who congregated mostly in Grace and went on a renaming spree, were big on flowers, even bigger on herbs.)

There is only one room, but the closet is large enough to secrete a foam pad and sleeping bag that allow me to crash if I don't feel like moving on. There's also a Styrofoam cooler and a little fridge behind the bookcase, where I keep enough food and drink to carry me through an in-house lunch or dinner. And there's a bathroom almost big enough to let you sit down on the toilet without banging your knees against the sink.

What there isn't is a TV. I get my news via radio or newspaper. Despite my chosen profession, I OD quickly on violence, and pictures like those of the victims of Seattle's last serial killer were gruesome enough in halftone in the *Times;* I didn't need Technicolor. The sicko, media-dubbed the Crucifixer, had not been content to rape and strangle his three victims; he'd laid their bodies on a makeshift funeral pyre with a crucifix in their folded hands and burned their bodies to ashes. And was never caught.

My second home is primarily a weekend residence, in the mainland city of Emerald, with my lover, Gray—well, his given name is actually Timothy Gray, but I've never heard anyone call him that. He holds the post of Chief of Police there, the result of a maneuver that backfired. We had both been on the Chicago police force, me as a rookie, he as Chief of Detectives, Homicide. We met in the aftermath of my rape; but that connection was not why I joined the force. I pretty much served as my own detective on my case, tracking down my assailant. So I figured I could do the same for others.

Gray was never that crazy about my being a cop; so when I took a bullet in my twelfth month on the force and he could not dissuade me from continuing in the profession, he wangled himself a job offer as Chief in the smaller, safer city of Emerald in western Washington. But doggone, they still had this minimum-height requirement for their officers—something defeated in Chicago before my time.

Yeah, right.

Truth was, though, I'd about had my fill of Chicago by then. Not to mention the hierarchy of the heavily male police force. So I let him talk me into taking a look at Emerald; and while he was bonding with the boys in blue, I took myself a ferry ride across the channel and fell in love with an island. Two months later I was flying solo as a Washington-State-certified private detective—arguably a more vulnerable position than being *e pluribus unum* on a police force.

So while Gray and I get to see each other less often

than we'd like, for now this feels like where I want to be and what I want to be doing.

It's in Home Number Three that I spend most of my nights—a funky little van/camper tucked into the woods out back of the cabin my friend Free is renovating.

I tend to horde my savings against lean times, but this was a deal I just couldn't pass up. I first saw the thing parked on a scrubby lawn before an even scrubbier shack in a low-rent enclave of Port Angelina. The various bright hangings draped at the windows of both van and shack suggested New Age occupation.

The vehicle in question had once been a commercial van, with the one windowless side meant to bear the name of the business. This one, however, had been painted lipstick red, with what looked to be lightning bolts in chrome yellow streaking diagonally across and bright blue stars scattered overall. The CAMPER FOR SALE sign suggested inquiring within.

It had never occurred to me to add such a vehicle to my resources, but I'd been tent camping in the woods behind Free's cabin, and the chill was starting to remind me that it was almost November, so I inquired within.

The owner, it turned out, was a wiry, wide-smiled kid of seventeen by the name of Leon Lopez, who had bought the van used (*well*-used, it appeared) and had done the conversion work himself—bypassing most codes, he hinted, in the interest of economy.

Leon's version of the pop-top had been created by a severance of the roof of the van that looked as though it had been done with a chain saw, the two-foot gap between covered with screening amply welded in place. I thought it was probably a bargaining point that few adult humans could stand erect in the height thus provided, custom-made as it seemed to be for Leon's five feet two or so; but the space was positively roomy for my own four-nine, so I chalked it up to serendipity.

The driving end of the van was separated from the living quarters by a midnight-blue velveteen drape, whose opening and closing Leon demonstrated with all the aplomb of a Vanna White. There was a kitchenette of sorts and a chemical toilet shielded by a shower curtain, but what really sold me was the setup in the rear. A double mattress rested on a raised platform just at the level of a two-by-four-foot horizontal window. The suspicious stains on the mattress suggested that replacement might be in order, but I could already picture myself curled up back there among a pile of pillows, gazing out at a sylvan scene or a coastal storm.

All Leon wanted for the van was enough to buy himself a new Red Devil motorcycle, so we struck a deal on the spot and I don't know which of us was more thrilled.

Since I didn't really plan to use the thing for transportation—my trusty Honda Civic serving that purpose well—I drove the van only around the block (perched on the edge of the seat to reach the pedals) and never followed up with anyone's mechanical assessment. What you don't know . . . Besides, questions might then come up regarding codes and registration and insurance; best to leave it a cabin on wheels in the woods.

I'd meant to paint over the mural, but I never got around to it and it's kind of grown on me. Besides, it's well-hidden in the trees from any curious eyes. So that's where I returned that night to mull over my new case in solitude.

As I stretched out on my lovely multipillowed bed,

I decided that the first enigma was Mary Alice herself. She certainly was holding something back, but did that signal deceit of any sort, or was it only her nature to hold herself in reserve? I'd had no sense of her lying intentionally about anything she'd told me, but her naïveté seemed extraordinary. Twenty-seven wasn't all that old, but it wasn't young either; yet it was hard to picture her interacting with others in any of the usual ways. She had a job—though if you thought about it, one's contact with the public must be limited in a dry-cleaning establishment. Maybe that was what she was comfortable with: clothes without people in them, tags with names and numbers.

I got out the letters and went over them again. The second one read:

> *You probly think Im weerd I dont just come up to you and say hi its me your Alice but realy I dont know what to say next to you. You look like such a proper young lady and all. I never was that. Thats what she always said she didnt want me being around you I wood make you bad too. And its true I been with lots of guys even then. But I didnt start it not what Im remembering not then not with him. And I been clean and working strate jobs four years now so I could be a good sister for you like we were. Do you remember? I want to be. Ill speak to you soon I promise.*
>
> *Your loving Alice*

The last just read:

> *I have to see you there are things I have to tell you. Please you must come to this restrant the Queens Rest you know where that is? Dont tell*

anybody just come at ten in the morning tomorrow.

The letter was postmarked March 13, for a rendezvous that was to take place six hours before Mary Alice received it.

The urgent tone of this one worried me. It was hardly a casual tête-à-tête being proposed, and I doubted that the writer would have missed it voluntarily. But that was a week ago. The trail would be pretty cold by now.

Outside, the wind gave the van an especially hefty battering, and the van creaked back. I looked up to see the lights go out in Free's cabin. A commonplace on the island: If the power doesn't go out at least twice a week in winter, we worry about global warming. I saw candlelight blossom in the cabin and felt a little smug. Since I don't have electricity in the first place, my kerosene lantern is already lit; a power failure just makes us all equal again.

I reached into the shelf on the right side of the mattress and pulled out a five-by-eight pad and pen. I try to make notes on anything that might have future relevance. Then I file them in one of those big brown accordion envelopes, a new one for each case. There are six pockets in the ones I use, and I label them *People*, *Locations*, *Possible Clues* (usually the tangible kind), *Hunches* (the intangibles), *Suspects* (who may get transferred from Category One), and *Data*, into which goes everything from family photos to copies of police reports. True, I haven't used all the pockets for every case, but I'm ready. Paperwork isn't my specialty—I prefer to be in action—but at least it helps organize my thoughts.

I peeled a white two-by-five label from its backing

and affixed it to the front of a new file, writing *Mary Alice Abbott* in Flair black script across it. Then I began writing up the people:

> Mary Alice Abbott, 27, 900 Glass Avenue, Grace
> Shirleen Holman Abbott, mother, age uncertain, same address
> Harley Abbott, father, age unknown, address unknown
> Alice Abbott, sister, age unknown, address unknown, past or present
> Wendell Holman, uncle, age uncertain, 26 Skyline Drive, Emerald

Age was clearly a fuzzy area in this family. Mary Alice seemed to be certain only of her own and looked alarmed that I would pursue the subject, particularly with regard to her mother. "I don't even know when her birthday is," she told me. "I know my uncle's is the seventh of September and that he's a couple of years younger than Mother, but he looks older and she won't let him say. I just put eleven candles on his cake every year, that's how many fit."

I jotted this down dutifully, along with whatever else she'd told me about any of them, which amounted to precious little. Even Mary Alice took up only three sheets, the rest one each. I filed Harley under *Suspects* and the rest under *People* and made a mental note to focus on filling out their profiles at my next meeting with Mary Alice, scheduled for 10:00 A.M. the next morning at The Queen's Rest restaurant.

Then I blew out the kerosene lamp and let the wind-stirred rustle of pine boughs against the roof, and their blown fragrance through the screens, lull me to sleep.

CHAPTER 4

WHEN I SLEEP IN THE WOODS, I look forward to my morning run on a path spongy with rotted leaves and bark, wheeling around tree trunks and jumping fallen logs to a dirt road that dead-ends in a stand of bamboo dense to the point of impenetrability.

My self-made path meets the road at the site of an abandoned cabin, its clearing nearly fully reclaimed now by the forest. A sign next to it, crudely lettered on a board nailed to a post, reads BARBER LANE.

Since there is only one such road into the woods for miles around, I have assumed that the occupant of that lone cabin used to be the community's barber, made obsolete as towns sprang up, with vehicles to get to them. Whatever it once was, no one could inhabit the place now: The frame lists hard to starboard, and half the tin roof has crumpled into the interior.

Yet the morning after my first meeting with Mary Alice, as I drew parallel to the cabin, I thought I caught a glimpse of movement through one of its broken windows. I stopped to stare for a moment but saw only a glint of morning sun off a rough edge of the shattered glass. I did my usual U-turn at the bamboo and ran back, thinking nothing more of it until late that night.

* * *

I'd set the time and place for our second meeting at the same hour and locale Alice had chosen for the sisters' first rendezvous. I wasn't sure what significance either had, but her note had been so insistent that I thought it was a place to start. Alice had used the term "this restrant," which suggested to me that she was currently familiar with the place, might even be working there. Ten o'clock would be a time after breakfast and before lunch that might provide a staff break into which a quick meeting could be fit.

The Queen's Rest is a pricey restaurant mounted on a bluff overlooking Angelina Bay. It is just far enough from populous centers that it sees little of the daily business-lunch trade; but when an up-and-comer wants to woo a new client or show off the island to a mainlander, he heads for The Queen. It's also a popular lunch spot for idle wives, and I've heard there are private rooms in the back you can reserve for yourself and your illicit other, though I've had no cause to check it out.

I met Mary Alice in the lobby. She was there when I arrived at 9:50, looking no less tense than she had the day before.

I'd already given the place the once-over from the outside, slowing at the crest of Pike Drive and cruising the parking lot, peering into cars to see if I could spot anyone peering back. But the place seemed all but deserted, the dozen or so cars mostly grouped at the far end of the lot, probably designated for staff so the paying customers had fewer steps to walk in bad weather.

Today's sky was moving in that direction, a faint drizzle having begun as masses of ash-gray clouds moved in, herded by the wind like a flock of dirty sheep.

The building was gray stone, its ambience sort of a cross between a Moorish castle and a country club—a new ediface trying to look old. I had seen it only from the Port Angel waterfront, looming majestically at the crest of the bluff. From that distance one could mistake it for a manor house of the aristocracy if not the queen, but it did not bear closer scrutiny. Still, I tried to think charitably: Maybe its aspect lightened with more sunlight or the evening glow of lamplight from the bulbs plugged into the peaks of the crownlike portico.

The lobby was livelier but no classier, furnished with distressed antiques that couldn't seem to settle on what century they would imitate. Bloodred drapes hung at the floor-to-ceiling windows that flanked the entrance, matched by red runners of carpeting laid over nubby gray wall-to-wall like a diagram to direct traffic. I kept waiting for a madam to appear from behind a beaded curtain and ask our pleasure of companions for the evening.

Mary Alice was registering none of it, her gaze flitting distractedly from object to object as though expecting one of them to dissolve into the form of her sister. Without thinking, I offered her my arm, as you would to one elderly or infirm, and we proceeded through carved double doors to the inner sanctum of the place.

The sign inside said, PLEASE WAIT FOR THE HOSTESS TO SEAT YOU. But there was no hostess in sight and no tables occupied in the dining area, roped off from us by red plush swags anchored with gold-tone hooks to a pair of gold-tone posts that looked heavy enough to withstand an invasion. I surreptitiously nudged one with my index finger, tilting it without effort. So much for fortifications.

Through an archway to our right lay the bar,

which was not blocked off but was so dimly lit, the gloom itself might give one pause. On the left, just beyond a hostess stand of faux teak, a muffled clatter drifted through wide swinging doors, signifying a kitchen more focused on preparation than service.

It seemed clear that the place was not open for business at this hour, a further shoring to my notion that Alice might be staff. The thought prompted me to remove the golden hook from the golden post and guide my client past it and into the farthest, dimmest corner of the dining room.

Mary Alice made protesting noises but allowed herself to be pulled along, having the sense to whisper as she said, "Are we allowed to do this?"

"Probably not," I said, and kept on going. "If no one's around, then no one's bothered," I said as we seated ourselves. "I'd like to keep an eye on the room while we talk, just in case."

"In case?" she said. "You mean if we see Alice, don't you?"

"Exactly."

I pulled a pad and pen from my bag and prepared to record Mary Alice's answers to my questions. But I'd gotten no further than "Tell me about your mother" before a woman with elegant bearing emerged from the bar area, her long filmy skirt swaying about the ankles of her high-heeled boots.

She was aimed for the hostess booth but stopped midstride as she spotted us and altered her path in our direction. I put on my most winning smile in preparation.

She began to speak before she reached us. "I'm afraid we're closed for another hour still," she said, consulting a rhinestoned watch on her left wrist. "If you'd care to wait in the lobby . . ." Her arm made a graceful arc in the direction from which we'd come.

Mary Alice was already on her feet, so I rose as well. "Actually," I said, "I'd appreciate a moment of your time." I was in actress mode, modulating my voice to match hers; I hadn't been a theater major for nothing. "We're looking for a friend," I said. "A waitress here? Alice . . ."

I looked at Mary Alice, realizing suddenly that I didn't know what last name her sister might be using. She was staring at me with equal confusion. I finessed. "I don't know whether she's going by her maiden name. Abbott?"

"Alice Abbott," the woman replied, with just a note of tartness in her voice. "She did start with us. Several weeks ago. But it didn't work out."

I couldn't speak for a moment, my brain taken aback at our quick success. "Do you happen to know," I said, "where she was living or where she might have gone?"

The woman was looking as though we'd taken enough of her break time.

"We could wait awhile," I said, "if you have other things you need to do now."

She seemed to be weighing which would be more burdensome to her. "I'll see if I can find anything," she said finally. "If you'd care to wait in the lobby."

We followed her back the way we'd come, Mary Alice gripping my forearm with a force I was sure would leave a bruise.

The wait seemed interminable, but our grudging hostess eventually returned with a mailbox number and a Port Angelina zip code written on a logoed pad. "This is all she gave us," she said, "for the W-2."

"May I ask why she was let go?" I said, knowing I was pushing our luck.

She regarded me for a moment and apparently decided on honesty. "She was clumsy," she said. "Not just physically, but socially. We thought she had potential, but—" She tore the sheet off the pad with a flourish and extended it. I reached into the front pocket of my shoulder bag and fished out a card, which I exchanged for her note. "Thank you for your time," I said. "If you hear from Ms. Abbott, please give me a call."

I left her with The Look on her face as I guided Mary Alice out the door.

"What we can do," I said to her as we hustled through the accelerating rain, "is stake out the post office while we talk. I need more background on your family and anyone else you can think of whom Alice might have contacted since she's been back." I knew it was highly unlikely that the woman would come for her mail just when we happened to be there, but Mary Alice looked as though she could use a dose of hope and I needed the information.

My client followed me down the hill in her aging Chevy, then through a few false turns while I tried to locate the post office from faint memory, having been there only once.

My knowledge of Port Angelina has gaps. A good three times the size of Grace, Port Angel is the east-side entryway to the island, the favored path of Seattleites and all those north. Two of my past clients lived there, but since their runaways were clearly off the island, I'd done no searches in the town itself and had to do some zigging and zagging to guess my way along. I began to think I should have let Mary Alice lead; maybe she knew the town better than I, since she worked just up the highway. But I couldn't really picture the woman leading anyone anywhere. A bad business, dependence, whether you call it protection or not. It had been the fond hope of my own parents, but luckily it was foiled early.

I finally found the station on Granger, just west of Speers, and lucked out finding two spaces in the metered parking lot on its south side. I locked my car, fed the meter, and joined Mary Alice in her faded blue Nova. It was better positioned to keep an eye on the front door. Besides, in her car you could actually see the seats. My little Civic had become overstuffed with files, maps, books, fast-food cartons, and wardrobe changes. A by-product of driving solo, and usually on business.

I hauled out my pad and pen and began the interview again, though most of my questions got directed to Mary Alice's profile, so fixed was her gaze on the post office entrance.

Completed only last year, the building is red brick with white trim and inexplicable iron bars at the windows, as though the place doubled as a jail—which to the best of my knowledge it does not. My only previous visit was to mail a package before I caught the ferry to the mainland, and I'd encountered nothing out of the ordinary: rows of individual brass boxes, in-town and out-of-town slots, and the usual inadequate single table that all must share to assemble their packages and lick their stamps.

The rain was coming heavier now, the wind strong enough to make the drenched American flag out front unfurl in almost horizontal snaps that could be heard even with our windows rolled up tight. I tried to remember whether I'd battened down all the hatches on my camper.

"Your mother," I said to Mary Alice's left cheek. "You said she uses her maiden name? Holman?"

"One *L*," Mary Alice said automatically. "She says she never should have given it up."

"So she doesn't use Abbott at all? Has she ever used it?"

"I guess so," Mary Alice said, "when they were married. But she's been Holman as long as I can remember."

"But you use your father's surname."

Mary Alice glanced back at me, her expression shrewder than I'd seen it. "She probably wanted to be sure people knew I was legitimate. When she's mad, she says, 'At least I got you a proper father, didn't I?' "

I was rerunning that statement through my brain when suddenly Mary Alice jerked open her door and took off at a dead run toward the post-office lawn.

I did a double-take in that direction and saw a woman in a bright red raincoat chasing a matching hat across the grass, her long russet hair whipping in the wind like the tail of some tropical fish. If Mary Alice's speed surprised me, the other woman's did more: Even from this distance I could see that her shiny red rain boots had a good three inches of heel on them.

I opened the door on my side and joined the pursuit.

When I got there, the woman had the hat by the ties and was trying to hold the box she carried against one hip with her elbow so she could free her hands to retie the hat. Mary Alice had caught up with her but missed a beat or two just staring before she thought to help.

I was about to take the package myself when Mary Alice came alive and reached both hands for it. The young woman smiled and let her take it, apparently unruffled that two crazy people had just torn across a parking lot to be of dubious assistance.

She could not have been more than twenty, with the pale skin and impudent freckles of a natural redhead. And though she took the time to retie her hat in a full bow, she finished long before Mary Alice was finished staring. But she said only, brightly, "Thank you," and reversed her course toward the porch of the building, where she passed inside.

Only then did Mary Alice turn and head back toward the car, with me trailing.

"Did you think it was Alice?" I asked her when we were back out of the rain.

"I don't know," she said. She said it twice: "I really don't know."

CHAPTER 5

I'D FELT RESTLESS AND DISSATISFIED when I'd parted company with Mary Alice. The girl in red had seemed to send her back into herself, and I saw we'd covered all the ground we were going to for that day. I let her return home, agreeing to meet for dinner the next evening. Having missed one day of work already, Mary Alice didn't feel she could risk another, and there was ground I could cover without her—paper trails to follow, background checks to make. We agreed to meet at The Blue Heron at six the next day.

Which reminded me that I'd had precious little to eat in this one. Granola and oranges after my run that morning had not been followed by the expected lunch at The Queen's Rest, and I was ready for a king-size meal. So I headed for my favorite dive, The Galleon, on the back streets of Grace.

The Galleon wastes little effort on atmosphere. A few moldy fishing nets are draped from high beams I've always suspected of harboring bats—a theory I've hoped never to verify. The rain-guzzling cinder block frame of the building is in perpetual war with its inner drywall, the latter demonstrating its defeat in the array of Rorschach-like stains that pattern its face. But one bowl of The Galleon's "sea chowder" and a mug of its hot buttered rum, and you are hooked for life.

I waved to Eduardo, the owner-chef, through the window to the kitchen and kept on going to the backmost table. I had thinking to do. There was something about this case that felt charged beyond the boundaries of its known facts. Mary Alice's troubled feelings ran deep, and seemed as much a mystery as those of her sister. Not to mention the mother's reported behavior and Alice's charges against "him"—Mary Alice's father presumably.

It was frustrating to get so little solid information from the client. It was like listening to a radio station that is barely coming in, hearing tantalizing moments that then turn to static. And what about the others' versions of the story? I was ready to nominate the lot for Dysfunctional Family of the Year, sight unseen.

I drowned my nagging questions in chowder, hush puppies, and loganberry pie, then put in a call to my answering machine at the office. I punched in 575, my access code, and listened to its single message—from a birth mother who had not been at all certain she wanted to be found. She was calling to say things were going well, and thanked me for my efforts. At least some stories had happy endings, I thought, though my instincts told me that this one might have more potential for tragedy.

I felt too restless to devote the rest of the afternoon to paperwork, so I aimed my little Honda for Brandy Point, a narrow peninsula just above Grace, and took a walk out on its seawall to the defunct Second Mate's Lighthouse.

The rain had stopped, but bands of heavy cloud cover kept the sky as dark as evening, and the wind was still whooping it up as it carried the storm out to sea. I stripped off my socks and sneakers and left them on the beach, the better to negotiate the slippery rocks. Though the wall rises a good ten feet above the high-tide waterline and is at least three feet wide, the relentless spray as wave hits rock keeps the surface perpetually slick, adding that edge of danger to a jaunt that is really quite safe.

The swishing of the surf was lovely so close below me, and I embraced what I could reach of the dark lighthouse and sidled around it, then lowered myself into a familiar wedge between two boulders to sit so my feet could play footsy with the licking waves.

What is it about water that's so soothing to the human soul? It's one of the many perks of island living: You're never more than a few minutes from the sea. Unfortunately, frantic city dwellers in a widening radius have been discovering just that, and Prince Island tracts with "watr vu" have climbed to six figures, the first digit climbing still.

I breathed deeply of the tart salt air. Across the Strait of Juan de Fuca to the west, the small peninsula town of Port Juniper was only a tiny cluster of structures against a vast backdrop of evergreens, with Emerald and Seattle to the east reduced to a far-off haze. On my first trip to the Northwest some fourteen months before, I had felt an immediate sense of physical relief as the plane descended into a landscape of forest and ocean that still dwarfed the settlements of human encroachment. It had revealed a conviction I didn't know I had: that Nature, capable of its own mighty upheavals certainly, is still a more trustworthy environment in which to live than the airless, colorless cityscapes into which people have crowded themselves like so many mice in a cage. In clinical trials, I recalled from college psych, mice kill each other and themselves under such conditions. It had been my experience during my years in Chicago that people did the same. So while I'd fussed about the lack of high drama in my Prince Island caseload, I'd been reassured by it too—as reassured as I now was troubled by aspects of this new case.

I went over it again: What did I know and what did I need to know?

Father: Harley Abbott; accused by Alice of sexual abuse; middle name, age, and address unknown. Left the family or was evicted when Mary Alice was almost three. Need to know: *everything*.

Mother: Shirleen née Holman, turned Abbott, returned Holman. Evicted the daughter, then the husband. Had she known what was going on? Who was the woman she'd sent Alice to? With what agreement? Had she kept contact since? Need to know: plenty. Even her relationship with Mary Alice—All I really knew about their bond was that word that kept cropping up: *protection*.

Alice Abbott: older sister, but by how much? Again that word: *protection*. Against what or whom? Why exactly had she been sent away, and where had she been the past twenty-some years? Why had the rendezvous with her sister at The Queen's Rest failed? And most importantly, of course: Where was she now?

Then there was the uncle: one Wendell Holman.

That's when the name hit me. He must be the same Wendell "Windy" Holman who dished out the jokes with the weather on Emerald TV, Channel Four. One more jolly weatherman in that brotherhood of jolly weathermen who seem to feel compelled to provide chuckles along with their forecasts. It had always struck me as curious that every local TV news team I'd ever seen had a jocular weatherman. The same didn't seem to be true of weatherwomen; the few of those I'd seen had run more to blondes than clowns. "Windy" Holman. Small world. But I could see why Mary Alice's face brightened whenever she mentioned her uncle: Neither Mom nor Dad seemed to have been a barrel of laughs.

It was nearly four when I got back to my car, but my head felt close to clear, my senses alive. I headed into the office, where I committed my mental notes to paper, caught up on some other work, then joined my friend Ellie at The Blue Note to hear a singer she'd been raving about.

So it was a little after ten when I pulled up to my camper. Free's cottage was dark and her truck gone. I had just climbed out of the old Civic, holding my I-am-one-of-you silk dress as far from my grubbies as my arm could reach, when I thought I smelled smoke.

I cocked my head in that birdlike way people do when their senses are alerted. Then I hung the dress on the handle of the door and circled the camper, peering into the woods beyond. I saw no flames, but that was definitely the direction of the smoke, little trailers of it rising like kite ribbons into the moonlit sky.

I took off running, heading in the direction of the smoke.

The direction of my morning run. The direction of the cabin.

That was when I remembered the glimpse of movement I thought I'd seen at the cabin's window that morning, and my chest contracted with dread. I wished I'd stopped to grab my gun. It was probably just kids carrying their vandalism of the cabin one step further. Still . . .

The smell of gasoline was getting stronger, my heart beating faster.

Then dread turned to cold fear as I broke into the cabin's clearing to see—not the ruins afire as I'd expected, but the cabin's ancient boards converted to a funeral pyre on which a body was burning.

He's come here! was my sole thought before pain splintered through my head and the curtain fell.

CHAPTER 6

THEY TOLD ME I'D DRIFTED in and out of consciousness several times before I finally woke. But the first thing I really remember is the sight of Gray's and Free's faces gazing at me with identical expressions, their eyebrows scrunched, three worry lines each rising from them. They looked so comical, I laughed out loud.

The lines erased and they slapped palms, as though it was they who'd succeeded in bringing me back alive. I didn't have the heart to tell them I had had no intention of dying; I was just resting. Probably.

They crowded to the bedside, Gray taking my hands between his, Free lightly touching the bandage that wrapped my head, as though feeling for a temperature.

"How long have I been out?" I asked through the muffle.

"Only a day," Free said. "And two nights."

Then I remembered. "The Crucifixer! Was it him? Did they get him?"

Gray's worry lines returned, and I realized he'd probably been hoping I would waken with the words, "Whoa, that's all the sleuthing for me!"

"Similar M.O.," he said. "Could be a copycat.

And no, he was gone when they got there. They're searching the woods." He squeezed my hand as though he could drain all such preoccupations from me like milk from a cow. "Forget it. It's not your worry now."

I turned my head—carefully—toward Free. "Was it you who found me?"

She shook her head. "Time I got home, it was all over. Somebody from Breadloaf Hill called 911 and reported seeing smoke."

"Squad car got there before the fire truck," Gray said, with just a tinge of pride for his counterparts on the island.

There was an annoying odor I'd been assuming was hospital disinfectant, until it came back to me: *gasoline*! "He doused me!" I yelled, my hands flying out of Gray's and snatching at the sheet, half-expecting to see the rest of my body swathed in bandages too.

"They reached you in time," Gray said.

"Yeah, you don't burn so good," Free said. "They been trying to get that smell off you, but it's a bitch."

I smiled in embarrassment at my panic and returned my hands topside, clamping them together to hide their trembling. "Be a helluva way to die, wouldn't it?" I said, with only a little squeak to my voice. "Who was she? Do they know?"

"They're trying to identify the body now," Gray said.

"That bastard. I was hoping he'd quit. It's been half a year since the last one."

"Instead, he moves here," Free said. "Damn! Soon as you think you left that shit behind, it follows you."

Free was referring to her recent exodus from Seattle. A whiz kid who'd gotten her Master's in Business at twenty-two and gone straight into Seattle's primo public-relations firm, Free had become disenchanted just as fast and left it all to open a used-book store in Grace. I'd met her by becoming her best customer, then friend, then neighbor when she invited me to camp on her back forty. As women who've chosen to live with a measure of solitude, I think both of us feel more comfortable knowing the other is nearby. Well, usually nearby.

"Freedom" is the latest in Free's choice of names. Born Bessie Smith Davis, Free in her teens rejected the name of that grandmother of blues singers, calling them collectively "those crybaby mamas addicted to men." Instead, she affirmed her African roots by taking the single name Asmara, after the city in Eritrea to which she'd traced her family. That was how she was known professionally, until she relocated to the island and adopted the name Freedom to celebrate her liberation of herself from the world of crass commerce.

"Okay, girlfriend," she said now. "Seeing as how you back in the land of the living, I got a shop to open." Free "talks white," as she puts it, whenever it suits her purpose. But given her druthers, she "talks soul."

"I'll call," she said, "see when they're ready to spring you, and we can plot our strategy for getting you out of here."

"Strategy?"

"They're keeping you out of the press," Gray said.

"Oh, God, the press!" I put my hands to my aching head. "Won't this be dandy for business: 'P.I. stumbles onto murder scene, promptly gets herself clobbered.'"

"Both the hospital and the police are saying your identity is being withheld for your protection," Gray said.

"My professional protection," I retorted, though

my heartbeat was saying that the threat to business was the less scary of the two.

"They're saying you're still in a coma," Free said.

I looked at them. "Was I?"

"Nothing that deep," Gray said, "but that's what they've been putting out, and they'll continue to as long as he's at large."

"Might be one long coma," I said.

"Might be."

"Then how do I get out of here?"

"Through trickery and stealth," Free said, grinning wickedly.

I did a Groucho with my eyebrows. "Two of my favorite companions," I said.

That's when I noticed there was some role reversal going on here: two women trying to reassure a man with macho cheer.

Gray wasn't going for it though. "She'll be coming home with me," he said to Free, in that even voice he uses to discourage argument. "I think the farther from this scene, the better."

I sighed. Apparently the honeymoon between them was over and their territorial battle had returned. Why can't you make the people you love love each other?

I gave him a look he was familiar with. I knew his concern was as genuine as his love, and probably more justified, but nobody tells me what to do. Nobody.

"Honey, I've gotta stay on the island," I said to him, surprised at how softly it came out. "I've got a job to do, and my client's freaked."

"As freaked as the Crucifixer?" he said, his lips gone thin with tension. He knew he didn't stand a chance of changing my mind, but he had to give it a try.

"If there's anyplace the creep *won't* be hanging

around, it's Shepherd's Woods," I said. "If he's managed to get out, he certainly won't come back. It's probably Cop City there by now. Couldn't be safer."

"You're not going back to that . . . happy-wagon," he said. It was a statement, a last resort.

I grinned. " 'Happy-wagon'?"

That got a small smile out of him.

"Besides, she'll be staying with me," Free said. "This kind of thing may be all in a day's work to you two, but personally, I could use a little P.I. protection. And two guns are better than one."

That was the first I'd heard she had a gun. Though maybe it was only conceived for the purpose.

Gray's beeper went off, even its small, shrill sound making me jump. He had to get to a phone but did not choose the one beside the bed. He stood looking down at me for a moment with his soft blue-gray eyes, then sighed. "You'll do what you want, of course," he said. "Just do me a favor? Don't try to save the world all by yourself?"

It seemed a reasonable request.

They left together, and I was reminded to check my own machine. Mercifully, there were no messages. I lay back and closed my eyes. Close calls can really wear you out.

All too soon, a young sallow-faced doctor arrived, with two nurses in tow—in order to check me out, he said self-importantly, before he'd let the police in to interview me.

But after some more prodding of my head and peering into my eyes with a blinding penlight, I was declared ready to be back among the living.

The two officers who came in were familiar to me. I'd heard their voices in the hall with Gray's while I was being examined, and gathered from what I could make out that they were asking him not to be present at the interview. Perhaps, I thought, to ensure that my story would be fully candid, without pulled punches for the anxious lover.

"So, Piper. You nearly made Number Five."

The man with the mammoth tact was Sergeant E. Cecil Gersch, called "Easy" at his insistence. He means well. Or so I keep telling myself. Gersch is one of those veteran cops who are still uncomfortable with the idea of women in the business and overcompensate by coming on too chummy. But then, his whole shtick is chummy. In his mid-fifties, all ruddy skin and rounded contours, the man looks born to play Santa Claus. Which he does, in fact, each year at the Island County Patrolmen's Party for needy kids. With his heavy thatch of white hair, the conversion takes only the addition of a beard and a red rubber nose to cover his own, which has been broken so often it now hooks sharply to the right.

We did not get off to a great start, Easy and me. I'd been in business for a month or so before we were introduced at a reception for the new Grace Tourism Coordinator. Whereupon he put a hammy arm around my shoulders and said, "I hear you're a feisty one."

Talk about pushing a button. For me, the *F* word is *feisty,* followed closely by *spunky* and *spitfire.* I mean, have you ever heard anyone say "that feisty Terminator" or "spunky Sly Stallone"? "Some spitfire, that Superman."

Needless to say, Gersch did not get the warm-and-fuzzy response he was probably going for. He was lucky not to get a kick in the shins. We have both been working on rapprochement since though. I can't do my job without good working relations with the police, and Gersch is not as foolish as his good-old-boy act might make him appear. So I try to keep my ears open and my big mouth shut. I may never be sure that the Emerald officers don't treat me with respect only because of my association with their chief, but on the island I'm on my own. And over the course of a few cases, they seem to be coming around.

Number Two in the officers' duo was Hart Burrows, as much a sphinx as Easy is a clown. I don't believe I've ever seen the man grin, or lose his temper, or show any sign of uncontrolled emotion whatever. But on this occasion his green eyes were as bright as Easy's blue; these guys, I thought, are hyped. Our little island was making the big time as the new home of Seattle's serial devil, and they were fairly spouting adrenaline.

"You guys got hospital duty?" I said.

"Everybody's been called in on this one," Easy said. "Grace, Port Angel, Sweetbay, even the Base. Sheriff's men are all over those woods right now lookin' for the guy. But if you ask me—and nobody did—I think he's long gone. I mean, would you stick around until the whole island got there? He had a good fifteen, twenty minutes to get away before backup arrived.

"Anyway, they sent us here to wait till you woke up, see what kind of ID you could give us."

"Well, sorry to disappoint you, guys, but the only description I've got is that the guy wields a mean 'blunt instrument.'"

"You got no look at him at all?" Burrows asked in obvious disappointment. They had that eagerness about them kids get on a scavenger hunt, wanting to be the first team to the prize. I wondered whether that meant they now saw me as one of the Grace Team. An ironic accomplishment.

" 'Fraid not. I followed the smoke, saw the pyre and the body, then—" I mimed a karate chop in the air.

"And that was what—ten o'clock?" Easy said.

"A little after, I think."

"How far burned was the body when you saw it?" Burrows asked.

"I couldn't really tell, I wasn't that close. But it couldn't have been burning too long, or there'd have been some smell, wouldn't there? Of burning flesh? I imagine I'd have noticed it earlier." Before I went barging into the scene, I added silently.

"Wait a minute." I pushed myself more upright in the bed. "The gasoline. That's what I smelled most, that and the smoke. The Crucifixer's never used gasoline. Does that mean this one's somebody else?"

The two officers exchanged a quick glance but said nothing.

"Hey, guys," I said. "I just about got roasted. Let's not be coy with the details, okay?"

"Once," Burrows said. "When the wood was wet, like last night. They kept it out of the papers."

"To distinguish copycats," I said. "What about the crucifix? Did she have one?"

Gersch suddenly found his shoes needful of scrutiny, and Burrows might as well have been a statue.

"Dammit . . ."

"No," Burrows said. "She was stabbed with a nail in the heart. The M.E. thinks after she was strangled, but before she was burned."

That stopped me. I gotta admit, that stopped me. I suddenly found my hands covering my chest and my breath in remission.

"Let's go over the time frame," Gersch said, perhaps wanting to distract me. "When did you first smell the smoke, and how long did it take you to get there?"

I pulled myself back into information mode. "I think it was just after ten when I got in, and it probably took me fifteen minutes or so. My usual run is about twenty each way, running easy." Then I remembered. "Actually," I said, "I may have noticed something before last night. That morning."

I put a hand to my throbbing head, feeling dizzy.

"Would you like to take a break?" Gersch asked.

I shook my head, took a deep breath. "I go by there every day on my morning run. That morning—yesterday?—I thought I saw movement in the cabin. Something. But I decided it must have been a trick of the light and didn't investigate."

"Probably a good thing," Burrows said, "the kind of pervert we're dealing with."

"The cabin was intact then, or as much as it ever was. When I saw it that evening, it had been half-dismantled. But with that side already caved in, it wouldn't necessarily have taken him a lot of time to get the wood he needed for the fire."

"So either the man didn't have his victim yet that morning or he was taking his time with her," Burrows said evenly.

I didn't respond, except with a mental shudder.

"Was there enough of the body left, then, to identify?" I said, relieved not to hear my voice quaver.

"It's in Forensics, King County," Burrows said.

"You must have interrupted him early enough to shortstop his process," Easy said. "Maybe this time we'll get lucky."

Tell that to the victim, I thought.

CHAPTER 7

IT WAS ONLY AFTER THEY'D LEFT, around ten-thirty, that I thought to call Mary Alice at work and explain that I'd been unable to make our dinner meeting the evening before. An accident, I'd tell her. One I didn't want to advertise, for professional reasons.

I don't know what I'd expected, but I guess I was unprepared for the sullen indifference with which she took the news of my hospitalization. I came very close to telling the woman to find herself another investigator. Maybe to her I was just another no-show in a long line of those she felt abandoned by, but I wasn't in the mood for tolerance. I made a decision on the spot: I would quit trying to decipher reality through Mary Alice's eyes. I told her I wanted to meet the family.

There was such a long silence, I wasn't sure she was still on the line.

"How do you mean?" she said finally.

"Well, have me over for dinner."

"At the house?"

"Sure."

"But who would I say you were?"

"A new friend. Hell, I don't know. But I think this investigation would go a whole lot faster if I at least met your mother, started to form some impressions of my own."

"Well, I guess. . . ."

"They're letting me out at noon. Could you swing a dinner invitation for this evening?"

"Gee, I don't know. . . ."

Mary Alice was never going to win any medals for spontaneity or decisiveness. But then, I wasn't going to get one for patience either. I couldn't really know, I told myself, what demons might have been resurrected by her sister's return. So I tried to soften my tone and reassure her that I would be the soul of discretion. Reluctantly, she agreed to dinner at seven. Now I just had to find a hat that would cover my bandage so I wouldn't freak them out with my Bride of Frankenstein impression.

They let me out at one—after midmorning rounds and a healthy lunch of dry fish patty, iceberg lettuce, and cherry Jell-O. I was ravenous for a Big Mac and fries. I wondered if I could talk Free, dietary snob that she is, into a quick stop at McDonald's, since we were already on the west side—the only source of fast food on the island.

There's an interesting east–west dichotomy on the island. Us Easterners (only twenty miles max from our western neighbors, mind you) think of ourselves as the good guys, the peacemakers; those on the western side, dominated by Orson Naval Base, are thought of (by us) as the militarists—more like "them" on the mainland.

The division came about naturally enough, I guess, when the Navy moved in and set up its cannons on the west coast of the island at the outbreak of World War II, to protect the surrounding waters from invasions that never came. A generation later the peaceniks homesteaded more modestly on the eastern half of the island, bounded for much of its length by Shepherd's Woods.

In addition to locked gates and ticky-tacky housing, the Base brought fast food to the island, its influence spilling over into Sweetbay just to the south, the island's official capital and site of the Prince Island Mercy Hospital.

By the time I hit the streets, though, fast food was the last thing on my mind.

Free had appeared bearing a shawl and afghan, with a nurse pushing a wheelchair behind her. With nothing else to wear—my clothes of the night before having been confiscated by the police—I was bullied into sitting in the wheelchair in my open-air hospital gown, while Free wrapped the shawl around my head and shoulders, making me feel like an ancient from the old country, and the nurse spread the afghan across the lower half of my body. Then the three of us left the room like the Marx Brothers in drag.

The nurse, a petite blonde, poked her head out the door and actually spoke the words, "Is the coast clear?" before they pushed me out under the watchful eye of a uniformed police officer, who gave us a solemn nod as we emerged. An armed guard yet, I thought to myself; do I get one of these at home too? If they were trying to scare me, they weren't doing a bad job.

Several hallways, elevators, and lookouts later, I was bumped in the chair down a loading ramp from a pantry smelling of cheese and hustled into Free's red Jaguar, which took off at her usual breakneck speed. Through Sweetbay, up #309 past Port Condor and around Shepherd's Woods, my nerves wound tighter with each mile until, as we pulled into the drive, I gasped at the sight of a figure emerging from the woods behind my camper.

"Sorry to frighten you," Karen Pasco said, bending toward the window I had not rolled down.

Her smile, I thought, did not look all that sorry.

The bonding that's supposed to take place between women in nontraditional professions never happened between Karen Pasco and me. She'd been a cop on the island—the only woman on the force—for nearly two years when I showed up, and from her chilly reception I suspected that she'd wanted to remain the sole exception in a man's world of crime control.

A striking woman with ink-black hair in a severe bob, Karen gets much of her five-ten height from her legs, which operate at a brisk, purposeful pace even if she's only heading for the water cooler. Her dark eyes and heavy brows give her a formidable look when it suits her, though I've seen her on formal occasions and she can do glamorous too.

"We're still securing the perimeter," Karen said when I'd opened the window a crack. "Every officer on the island has been out ever since you were found. We'll get him."

"Great," I said.

"I'm assigned to stay within sight of your . . . vehicle here. So you have nothing to worry about."

"Great," I said again. "Thanks." And Karen Pasco strode back to her post.

"Fool woman," Free said. "That man's long gone by now."

I didn't know whether to hope that was or wasn't true.

I got out my side of the car and headed for the camper, afghan wound around me. "I'll just get my things," I said, hearing my voice faint, as though it came from a long way off.

I stopped when I reached my car, near the van steps. Maybe I could find something suitable for the Abbotts' dinner in the clothes bag in the backseat, I thought. And Free surely must have an extra toothbrush.

I didn't hear Free until she was right beside me. "They've checked it," she said. "And don't forget the gun."

"Right."

I made my legs climb the steps. The door had no lock, and I'd never noticed how gratingly it creaked when you opened it.

My glance went immediately back to the bed. It looked the same. So why did it seem so much less inviting? "Damn," I said aloud, "the fucker's messing with my head."

I moved straight to the bed and snatched my gun from under some towels, checking the clip and jamming it home. I climbed on the mattress, peering out the back window as though the monster might be lurking there, just waiting for me to get him in my sights.

Instead, I saw Officer Pasco about fifty yards away, and I backed up quickly lest she turn and see me.

I banged around the place gathering underwear, a sweatshirt, jeans, and jacket, a couple of toiletries. I was almost out the door before I remembered the clothes I'd need for that night.

Cursing some more, I set the pile by the door and went back to drag my carton of respectable clothes out from under the bed platform, popping the four-way tuck and rummaging through until I came upon a gray wool dress with a white Peter Pan collar I didn't even know I had. Must have been one of my Salvation Army specials, I supposed, from the Junior Straightwear department. I grabbed some pantyhose and a pair of black patent-leather flats, stuffed the whole pile in a grocery sack, and headed for Free's. It was only 3:40; I could catch a nap on her couch if I slept fast.

CHAPTER 8

IF PRINCE ISLAND IS IMAGINED as a leaping dolphin, with Grace lying in the curve of its smile, then under its chin rests a little enclave of older, grander homes (pre-sixties but post-Victorian) in which the old-monied have taken refuge. Known as Serenity Shores, the thickly landscaped weave of streets is protected from further incursions by its waterfront boundary to the east and the twenty-acre Prince Island Sportsmen's Club buffering its rear.

I had recognized the Glass Avenue address Mary Alice had given me as being among the Serene and she had mentioned there was money in the family. Still, perhaps because Mary Alice herself seemed so solidly middle-class, I was surprised to see the stately Tudor that stood at that location. Set well back from the street and ringed by whitebark pines straight as soldiers, the place looked the picture of traditional elegance.

Shirleen was the second surprise. She answered the door herself, and for a moment I thought: This must be Alice come home. There was no way the woman before me could be Mary Alice's mother, let alone Alice's.

She waited several moments beyond polite to

smile. "You must be Mary Alice's little friend," she said.

The *L* word. Already I could see this woman and I were not going to be best buddies.

She didn't shake the hand I proferred, but she did step aside to let me in.

Shirleen Abbott came even closer to beautiful than her daughter did to attractive. She was delicately boned, a good foot shorter than Mary Alice (*Who's calling who little?*), and everything about her was smoother, brighter than her daughter. Her coloring, her gaze, her clothes were all fashionably young, as though the two had decided to switch generations. Her blond hair, expensively dyed, I was sure, was pulled up in a French twist, with curly little tendrils hanging down to frame her face and grace her neck. I could picture her spending hours each day at a gilded vanity, with hand mirror and curling iron, getting each curl perfectly corkscrewed and symmetrical around her head.

She wore a purple velvet lounging ensemble and matching flats with silver buckles that seemed never to have stepped beyond the front door. It was hard to believe that her figure had borne one child, let alone two, with its tiny waist and fat-free hips. And she'd taken all the advantage Mary Alice had not of generous breasts, the V neck of her outfit dipping between them to show just a tasteful amount of cleavage, accented by a silver chain.

What kept Ms. Shirleen short of gorgeous was a certain brittle quality about her. Though her features were delicate—a heart-shape face, tiny nose, bright blue eyes—they had an edge of sharpness that was unbecoming, as though they'd spent too many hours in one of those frowns your mother told you would freeze on your face if you weren't careful.

Then Mary Alice appeared behind her mother, as though to make the comparison complete. Her face was as immobile as ever, and she stopped well short of where her mother stood, as though to get closer would be crossing some forbidden line. "Dinner's almost ready," she said.

She was half-turned to go back to the kitchen when her mother said, "You haven't introduced us, dear," with an edge to her voice that more than canceled the "dear."

"Oh." Mary Alice turned back but did not approach. "Mother," she said, "this is Miss Piper. Molly Piper. My friend." She looked close to panic but continued. "Molly Piper, this is my mother."

Now the woman extended her hand, as though to do so before would have been an egregious breach of etiquette. "Molly," she said as her slim cool hand barely pressed mine.

"Mrs. Abbott," I said, realizing my mistake just a moment too late.

"Holman," she said. "Shirleen Holman," and waved away the beginnings of my apology. "Perfectly natural mistake," she said. Then, with a small mocking smile, "I tried marriage. I didn't like it."

Shirleen passed under an arch to my left, into the living room, despite Mary Alice's protest that dinner was imminent. "We have time for one glass of wine surely," she said over her shoulder without turning.

The timber-frame interior of the house gave it a medieval feel, its vaulted spaces crossed by dark-stained beams so heavy I had an impulse to duck—something I seldom have cause to feel. The woodwork in the living room, too, was dark, with a narrow balcony at the far end that looked purely decorative, since there were no stairs leading to it, only a small door in the facing wall. The drapes across the front of the room were drawn back, revealing three tall windows with the traditional diamond leaded hatchwork of windowpanes.

But the unmistakable focal point of the room was a near-life-size oil painting of the Madonna—sans child—rising four feet above the mantel of the fireless fireplace, ornately framed in what looked to be real gold. The figure, robed in vivid blue and crowned with a halo that turned the whole background silver, was impossible to ignore, so I complimented Shirleen on the painting as she gestured for me to sit in one of the wing chairs beneath it.

"Isn't she a blessing?" Shirleen responded from the bar under the balcony. "She's my most treasured possession. A genuine Beauvoire of course. My parents left her to me, along with anything else I possess." She gave a sigh, as though it weren't nearly enough, and I thought I saw her eyes turn misty, though it may have been only the wineglass she raised to her lips, handing me mine.

Despite the heavy framework, the rest of the decor in the room was surprisingly light, the stucco walls freshly painted cream, the wing chairs upholstered in a soft rose that matched the roses in the damask fabric on the couch that faced the fireplace. The hardwood floors looked original to the house and gleamed where not covered by the occasional Persian-looking rug.

I complimented her, genuinely this time, on her interior decorating. "Did you do it yourself?" I asked, and immediately regretted the question. What if she hadn't?

Luckily, she said yes, with a pleased smile, and we went in to dinner without any serious loss of ground.

Shirleen took the chair at the head of the table, her back to the kitchen's swinging doors, and motioned me with a nod toward the chair on her left. She stood until I had reached it, then sat—my cue to do likewise, I supposed. My mother always told me I'd regret my ignorance of etiquette.

Mary Alice waited until we were seated to bring in the dishes, one at a time. There was no cue to partake during this process, so I had plenty of leisure to take in the dining room decor.

The long oval table seemed to be rosewood, with six matching chairs, their seats covered in the same soft rose as the wing chairs. The same hardwood floors carried through the front hall and dining room, covered beneath the table with a thick oval rug in pinks on white. A floor-to-ceiling window facing the front of the house was hung in the same white raw silk as the table runner, the drapes pulled back by braided rose cords.

When all the food had been brought out in matching dishes of heavy silver, Mary Alice was apparently permitted to sit, and Shirleen reached out a hand to each of us, bowing her head and giving a rather lengthy thanks for all our blessings.

Then the silver covers to the dishes were removed to display a generous casserole of gooey red-white-and-green stuff that I guessed was spinach lasagna; a round bowl of baby peas and mushrooms; a basket whose steaming contents beneath a white linen napkin my nose identified as garlic bread; and a silver tray of raw vegetables that must have taken an hour to prepare, the carrot and celery sticks cut precisely with a serrated instrument, the radishes transformed by the knife into rosebuds, and the cucumbers into little boats holding a creamy pale yellow sauce. I began to wonder if Mary Alice had had to take time off from her job just for this.

I suspected that her mother had not joined her in the kitchen, from the way she surveyed each dish with a critical eye, Mary Alice studying her face for signs of displeasure. Then Shirleen gave an almost imperceptible nod, and the tension subsided a little from Mary Alice's shoulders, until her mother said, "Perhaps a spatula for the lasagna, dear. It's so frightfully messy if you can't cut a portion properly."

"Mmm, everything looks wonderful," I called to Mary Alice's retreating back as she reentered the kitchen, suspecting that mine were the only positive strokes my client was likely to receive that evening. She glanced back at me with a shy smile.

"I'm so glad I was able to get a fresh baguette," her mother said to me. "If you don't get them just from the oven, you might as well not bother."

"You have such a lovely home," I said, to change the subject. "Mary Alice said it's been in the family for some time?"

"Yes." She sighed. "My father had it built for us. It was completed just before my birth. Now these things are all I have left of him."

"Your parents are deceased?" I said, though I knew from Mary Alice that they were.

"Yes. It was a terrible accident. I was only thirteen." For some moments her face softened and her eyes lost focus. Then she touched her hair, bringing herself back to the present with a little shake.

"Have you always lived here then?" I asked, although the returned Mary Alice was giving me anxious looks, suggesting I should be more temperate with my questions. I figured it might be the only chance I'd get to probe though, so I continued. "You mentioned being married," I said. "I wondered if you continued to live here then."

She looked at me hard, as though it were a trick question. "Of course," she said finally. "This is my home. It has always been my home and always will be."

The finality of the statement was clear, so I filled my mouth with lasagna to keep it shut.

But after a moment she continued on her own. "My husband wasn't good for much," she said. "At least not in the practical ways of the world. I had to look out for myself, as I always have."

She gave me that little mocking smile again. I still hadn't figured out whether it was me or herself she was mocking, but I could tell that her monologue was launched, and I kept my peace. The more self-centered the object of your queries, I'd found, the more they'll reveal if you just let them talk. Periodic nods and "hmm"s and "that's interesting"s, and they can go on for days.

Shirleen sighed again. "I married very young," she said. "As you probably can tell from the age of my daughter."

I was about to break my own rule and jump on the subject, but I restrained myself.

"And I married for love, despite my mother's warnings." She drifted into reverie again, then said, "I thought I wanted children," in a tone that suggested she must have been out of her mind.

I glanced at Mary Alice. Her lids were lowered and her features registered no emotion.

"At least I had the presence of mind to draw up a prenuptial agreement," Shirleen said. "The man's got nothing I haven't given him."

Then, as though hearing herself sound less than ladylike, she laughed and poked at her lasagna with her fork. "Too much cheese binds up the spinach," she said lightly. "I can scarcely taste it." Then to me, "I've been taking a French cooking class at the Sweetbay Inn. It really spoils you for anything else."

I tried to drag her back to the subject. "What did your husband do?"

"Not much," she said sourly. Then, with more decorum, "My husband had his own transportation firm and made good money—when he worked. Unfortunately, he was too lazy or hung over most of the time to drive."

This woman, I thought, has just told me her ex was a trucker.

She sighed again. "Since he left us, a woman alone with a young child, my brother has tried to fill the void. He's been like a father to my daughter, bless his heart. I don't know what we'd do without him."

As though on cue there was the sound of the front door opening, and Mary Alice's head came up, an expression of pure joy on her face. I was stunned at the transformation.

She jumped up, with a bump to the table that set the ice in our water glasses tinkling, and headed toward the hall, stopped at the dining room arch by the figure coming in, who held out his arms to her. "How's my princess?" said the man I recognized as Weatherman Wendell "Windy" Holman.

He saw me then and looked somewhat surprised. "And who have we here?" he said to his niece, who had wrapped her arms around his ample waist.

Mary Alice went through her introductions again, this time remembering the designation of me as her friend.

"Well, welcome, Molly Piper," he said, with a hint of a bow. "Mary Alice doesn't often bring her friends home. I'm delighted to meet you."

The man was definitely the "Big Guy" his cocrew called him on the set. A good two hundred and fifty pounds worth was my guess, all of it softening with middle age. His hair was still thick, graying at the temples just enough to look distinguished. His mouth was wide, with smooth, almost feminine lips, and his eyes were as blue as those of his sister and niece, though the faint red lines that veined the whites—and the dark pouches beneath—suggested a love for the bottle. I guessed him at mid-fifties.

"And how is our queen?" he said, moving to kiss the hand his sister extended to him. It was the first time I'd noticed that the man limped; the TV cameras apparently averted their gaze from such imperfections.

Wendell started to lay his overcoat on a chair against the wall, then glanced back at his sister and returned to the hall, reappearing to take up what seemed to be his usual place at the table's foot. Mary Alice rushed to pass him the dishes of food, which he'd already complimented on the basis of aroma alone.

He was wearing what I think is called a smoking jacket, a rich burgundy fine-wale corduroy with satin shawl collar and cuffs, a shiny black-and-wine ascot tucked into its lapels. The smooth cream-color bowl of a pipe peeped from a tiny pocket on his left breast, looking so untouched by any match that I wondered whether the man actually smoked or carried it only for show.

Either way, I thought, these people sure knew how to outfit themselves for leisure. I could picture the two of them playing dress-up as children: "You be the lonely baron in the castle, and I'll be the lovely lost maiden who happens upon it."

And the less gainly Mary Alice? I wondered. What role was there for her in this little ensemble? It was stretching it to see her as the "princess" her uncle called her. Apparently, Alice and the husband hadn't suited their parts either. No wonder Mary Alice seemed to feel tenuous about her very existence.

"I'm glad you've decided to join us finally," Shirleen said to her brother, in a voice thick with sarcasm.

"You know I couldn't leave the station that night. I had the weather again at eleven. And with such a big story breaking, I was needed there," Wendell said, in a tone of lifelong forbearance. "I told you I'd come later if you wanted me to."

"And we wouldn't know if it was you or that devil at the door, would we?" Shirleen snapped.

Wendell chose to ignore the remark, and said, "I wish you'd just listen to me and give up this old house, come and live in Emerald with me. All that space just going to waste. Then I could keep a better eye on both of you."

Mary Alice looked eagerly at her mother; her vote was clear. But Shirleen's mouth had turned pouty, and she repeated the line about this being her home and always would be.

Wendell seemed to think the best he could do was to change the subject. "We've had more news about the second woman," he said cheerfully. "They're still not releasing her name or location, and she's still in a coma, but she's been moved off the island. So probably the killer's left too."

Shirleen had covered her ears with her hands at the

word *news*. "I don't want to hear it," she said, shaking her head.

Wendell turned to me. "My sister refuses to watch the news. Not even me. Out of sight, it seems, is out of mind."

I turned to Shirleen, ignoring her covered ears. "You really don't watch your brother on television?"

"Oh, we watch him all right," Mary Alice chimed in quickly. "When he does the six o'clock. I just have to tell Mother when the weather's coming on. She says there's nothing but violence on the news part and she doesn't want anything to do with it."

"She's right of course," Wendell said. "I often wonder how we in the media may be contributing to that. By showing so much violence day in and day out, we may be immunizing ourselves to it."

I then committed the grossest of faux pas. My tongue had discovered a piece of hard noodle in my mouthful of lasagna, and I'd raised my silky napkin to deposit the morsel surreptitiously, folding the clean part over the unclean. But when I was returning the napkin to its proper resting place, I overreached my lap and it dropped to the floor.

Murmuring something abject, I bent to retrieve it, only to have my hat slide off my head and join the napkin on the pristine carpet.

I really did not want to look up. I really just wanted to excuse myself and scramble out of the room on all fours. But that seemed less than professional behavior, so I plopped the hat back on my head and sat up again.

Shirleen was staring at me, as though some mangy dog had crashed her gate posing as a lovable stray. "Good heavens," she said. "What have you done to your head?"

Even in my dismay I noticed the wording, a thin slice of Mary Alice's daily bread.

"Just a stupid bump," I said. "It's nothing."

Then to my surprise, Mary Alice spoke up. "She fell," she said. "Really a bad fall. They had to take her to the emergency room."

I stared at her, failing for a moment to pick up my cue. Then I said, "I was remodeling a house. I went up, the ladder went down."

"That's why I invited her to dinner tonight," Mary Alice continued, on a roll. "I heard she'd gone into the hospital, and you know how that food is. So I called her and invited her to come for dinner when she got out."

"It was only a day," I said. "Overnight, really. But everything they say about hospital food is true. Mary Alice was so thoughtful to think of me."

Mother and Uncle had been watching this repartee from one to the other of us like a tennis match.

"How did you two meet?" Wendell asked. I probably only imagined that his tone was less than convinced.

"I take my cleaning there, to Redi-Clean," I said quickly, figuring it was my turn to save the day. "Mary Alice always has a kind word to say, so we just got to talking."

"And what do you do?" Shirleen asked me, her tone not dissimilar to her brother's.

"Remodeling mostly," I said. "Painting, stripping, roofing . . ."

"A little thing like you?" she said.

"Sure. I'm tougher than I look."

On that note I decided it was time to cut my losses and take my leave. I stood, touching the bandage where it now peeked out from beneath the hat. "I did promise the doctors an early night though. Thanks so much for dinner; it was lovely."

There were polite phrases all around, and within five minutes I was in my car, pulling around the white Lincoln I assumed was Wendell's, wondering if my cover stood a chance of surviving that little soiree.

CHAPTER 9

I FELT PHYSICALLY EXHAUSTED from the evening but still wired with tension, so I decided to pick up my mail and messages before heading home.

Outside of the four-block Parsley Street that represents the entirety of downtown Grace, there are no streetlights in the town and only minimal outdoor lighting on the houses—a product of the twin strivings for quaintness and political correctness. And 300 Dahlia, the converted Victorian in which my office is housed, is P.C. with the best of them. One faux carriage lantern at the door, with a bulb that couldn't be more than forty watts—that's it for the building, and for most of the rest of the block after office hours.

Ordinarily, I find that mellow, but I guess I was still a mite unnerved from my run-in with a killer, because I locked my car, even for the few minutes I'd be inside, and looked both ways like a first-grader before I crossed the one-way street.

The heavy oak door to the building has no lock, since all the inside doors do. I made a mental note to bring that up with Mr. Sullivan, the owner, at my next opportunity and pushed open the door, my senses wound tight as my bandage.

The overhead light on the second floor was on, so I didn't bother with flipping the first-floor switch, and I did the stairs at my usual run, my keys at the ready, and let myself into my office, locking the door behind me.

I was dearly hoping that this kind of paranoia was not the start of a lifelong complex. Once a P.I. loses her nerve, it's all over. Grace is not a high-crime town; few bother to lock themselves in or out of anyplace. But for now, I indulged a need for locks.

For once it was soothing to hear the ordinarily irritating strains of zither music coming from the apartment across the hall. The one-room efficiency is the building's only full-time residence; the other three "suites" are offices, nine to five. The tenant of the apartment, Tom (he pronounces it "T-om," like the chant, no last name,) is a teacher and nonstop practitioner of transcendental meditation. A nice kid, though his state of perpetual calm gets on my nerves after a while. Tonight, though, I could use all the calm I could get.

The trip at least proved worth it—a check among the junk mail and a lovely message on the machine from my mentor P.I. in Olympia: "Hello, Miss Molly, this is your neglected friend Simon Emmershaw calling Wednesday morning, wondering when you are going to grace us with your presence again. Call me at your liberty." I made a mental note to call as soon as I'd scheduled the trip I needed to make to Seattle—for Monday latest. My to-do list in that city was getting longer by the day; I could stay with Simon overnight and continue in Seattle the next day. I could use some of his veteran's wisdom on this one. For the moment I tidied up a bit of paperwork and left, locking the door and testing the knob to be sure all was secure.

Tom's screechy music had stopped, and I was halfway down the stairs when I heard a faint shuffling sound and stopped. I don't think I'd even have picked up on it if I hadn't been so edgy to begin with. I waited, holding my breath so it wouldn't interfere with my hearing. Nothing.

The area beneath the stairs is a storage closet for the use of the tenants. The only other occupant of the floor is Eugene Mulholland, Attorney-at-Law. He's a diligent chap who often works late, but tonight no light shone beneath his door. I was cursing myself for not turning on the first-floor overhead light, straining for any sound. Nothing.

I took two steps more, then stopped and listened again.

I was about to take another step, which would have put me on the fourth from the bottom, when a door opened above me and Tom's voice called, "Molly? Is that you?"

I have seldom been so glad to see anyone, however irrational the cause. As a protector, a skin-and-bones kid who specializes in keeping his eyes closed leaves something to be desired. But I was more than ready to take what I could get.

"When the music shut off, I thought I heard you in your office, so I was giving myself the five minutes to come out of it—you know, the state of oneness." Then he noticed the bandage; I'd left the hat in the car. "What's wrong with your head?"

"Nothing a little T.M. wouldn't cure, I'm sure," I said. "You haven't seen anybody hanging around the office, have you, the last few days?"

"Gee, no, but you know how it is when you really go under; you're not really aware of anything else."

A nice summary of my feelings against total self-absorption, I thought, then gave myself judgmentalism to work on for the next week's fault. "Well," I said, "see ya. I'll probably be in again tomorrow sometime," and gave him a wave.

I descended the rest of the steps, and my hand was on the smooth walnut knob, about to pull open the door, when I sensed another rustle of movement behind me.

I swung about quickly. But Tom was still at the railing, smiling down, one hand holding together the corners of his saffron loincloth. So I turned back to the door.

At most people's eye level, an oval pane of frosted glass is set into the thick oak door. In its center is etched the profile of a swan floating on an undulating suggestion of water. As I stared at it, I seemed to see a ripple of movement in the glass, as though the swan had begun to swim.

I turned again, peering through narrowed eyes at the dark triangle of the stairwell. I couldn't see the door to the closet, open or closed, and I pictured myself marching back there and checking it out. But some leftover childhood fear of monsters in closets and under beds kept my feet from moving. Instead, I pushed open the outer door and hurried as quickly as my dignity would let me back to the car, where my key fumbled with the lock infuriatingly before it opened, and I slid in, slamming the door and locking it behind me.

CHAPTER 10

I called my client at work at eight sharp the next morning and arranged to meet for an early lunch to plan our strategy. I was struck by the eagerness I heard in her voice compared to the trepidations she'd expressed whenever I asked her to vary her schedule in any way before. The brush with discovery had seemed to invigorate rather than inhibit her, and I spent the morning making lists of what we needed to know and where we might go to find it.

Mary Alice had suggested that we meet at the Fresh 'N' Fast deli in Hightower Square, about two miles past her workplace on #309. She was there when I arrived, hailing me from a back booth.

"How are you?" I asked as I slid in across from her.

"Good," she responded, and looked it.

"You were terrific last night," I said, and watched her perfect skin suffuse with pink.

"Do you think so?" she said. "I was afraid they could tell that I wasn't exactly telling the truth."

"Can they usually?" I asked.

She gave me that blank look of old before she said, "I don't think it's ever come up."

Now it was my turn to stare. "You mean you don't lie much?"

"Never that I can think of."

Oh, boy, I thought, time to corrupt the innocent. I leaned forward across the table. "Have you ever done any acting?"

Some fear returned to her eyes. "You mean like on a stage?"

"Or anywhere." I tried to choose my words carefully. "There is often some acting involved when you're on a case," I said. "What we need is information, and sometimes you have to persuade those who have it that you really need it."

"But if you *do* really need it, then it's not really acting, is it?"

"Well, no, I suppose not." The kid was sharp. "But it's not exactly pretense on the stage either. If you're supposed to cry, for instance, you can't just push a CRY button. You have to think about something that *is* really hurtful to you, so you can cry genuinely but on call."

"Have you done that, been an actress?" She seemed to peer at me with new interest.

"Well, some," I said. "Community theater. And in school." This was not an aspect of my background I wanted to emphasize. Theater people are generally thought to be flighty and undependable—not the sort of image a P.I. wants to project to her client. My B.A. in Theater is not framed on my office wall.

"We both did some acting last night," I said. "Do you think they believed us? What did they say after I left?"

"Nothing really. Only about the murders. That sort of thing really scares my mother to death."

"Join the club," I said. Then, to get us back on

track, "What we need now is information. On both your sister and your father. So we'll know how to look for them."

"My father?"

"Yes. The thing Alice came back to do—besides seeing you again—was to confront your father, right? Or at least find out something about him, to know whether her suspicions were correct. And I have a feeling—"

My presentation was interrupted by the waitress bringing us our menus. She continued to stand then, pencil poised over pad to take our orders.

"We'll need a little while to decide," I said to her, and she departed, though reluctantly. Maybe she's about to go on break, I thought, and doesn't want someone else to get her tip.

I put my palm to my forehead, which was still throbbing off and on, as though some memory were trying to break to the fore. "What was I saying?" I muttered.

"That you have a feeling," Mary Alice said.

"Right. What I suspect is that if Alice were still on the island, she'd have gotten in touch with you by now. Even if she'd changed her mind about meeting just yet. Since she hasn't, my guess is that she's found out where your father is and has gone there looking for him."

"Where?"

"Exactly: That's what we have to find out." Don't go dumb on me again, I thought.

"How?"

The waitress returned, and Mary Alice ordered absentmindedly without consulting the menu: turkey, lettuce and tomato on whole wheat, with iced tea. I'd been thinking more along the lines of corned beef and melted cheddar on an onion roll, then remembered that whenever I wasn't running, the pounds just piled on, so I seconded her order but opted for a Bud Light rather than the tea. After a moment of hesitation Mary Alice canceled the tea and doubled the beer, with a sly smile I took to mean that beer was one of the things a proper young lady didn't drink.

When the waitress had gone, I pulled my notepad out of my bag and faced it toward my client. "These are some of the places that have the sort of information we need," I said, "to find them both. The catch is that most of these bureaucracies will divulge information only to a relative—preferably one with the person's social-security number in hand."

I could see my meaning register with her, part anxiety, part excitement. "So you want me to . . ."

"Be yourself," I said. "Looking for the sister and the father that you haven't seen for twenty-odd years. Have you found any paperwork at all on either one?" She'd said no at our first conference, but I hoped she might have looked since.

"Not really. Anything like that, I think my mother'd keep in her own room, and I'm never supposed to poke around in there."

"Well, it's time to go poking," I said. "And we're talking every drawer, every closet, every shelf . . . But we can't wait for that now. This is Friday. We lost one day already while I was out. There are things we can try this afternoon and hope we get lucky. Otherwise, it will all be on hold until Monday. And every day Alice's trail gets colder. Is there any way you can take the afternoon off to help? Call in sick or something?"

I watched the doubt war with the desire on her face. Then slowly she said, "You know . . . every employee is allowed one personal half day a month. Or one full day every two months. We got that instead of a pay raise. But I've never taken any. In six years. So that half day I took on Tuesday? I said I was sick. But I didn't have to be sick. That could have been a personal half day. And so could this. I figure six years times six personal days a year: I have thirty-six days coming. Thirty-five after today. Don't go away, I'll be right back." And off she went in the direction of the pay phones over by the rest rooms.

I smiled to myself. I do like this job, I thought. Sometimes it's a bitch, but other times it is very, very satisfying.

Something was bothering me though, and I couldn't quite bring it into focus. Something about the restaurant? But I was sure I'd never been there before. I looked around. The decor was basic deli: meats and cheeses in a long glass case along the far wall, for those who want to pick their edibles like live lobsters. Busy staff dealing with the lunch rush, wearing white visors with the name Fresh 'N' Fast printed in red script across the band. Young mostly, only the middle-aged woman behind the deli case visorless, making those traffic-directing gestures that let you know she's in charge.

In the center of the large room, round chrome tables and white molded-plastic chairs were randomly arranged; red leatherette booths lined the rear and halfway up the other wall, breaking for the aisle leading to the rest rooms. The two pay phones were on the facing side, though a printed sign on one said OUT OF ORDER.

Beyond that, the only nontraditional equipment seemed to be the three video games hulking flank to flank in the corner to the left of the door. But their incessant electronic chatter was becoming commonplace most everywhere; I expected to find them in banks and libraries next.

Altogether, a pretty indifferent atmosphere to be triggering memories, the only form of artwork on the harsh pink walls the array of white poster-board rectangles beyond the deli case, all tilted at rakish angles, with a sandwich description hand-lettered in a different color of heavy felt-tip on each one. The Dagwood: salami, pastrami, pepperoni, swiss, American, bacon, and pickle relish on a twelve-inch hoagie, done in green. The Sailor: knockwurst, kraut, swiss, and Thousand Island on rye, in blue. The Sicilian: Genoa salami, ham, onions, peppers, provolone on an Italian roll, in orange. By the time the food came, I was drooling all over my list.

Mary Alice returned less jaunty-looking than she'd left.

"How'd it go?" I asked through a mouthful of muenster.

"He wasn't happy," she said grimly.

"But you got it? The afternoon?"

"I didn't back down," she said through a tight jaw.

"Awright!"

She gave me a rueful half smile and plucked a slice of turkey from her sandwich and put it into her mouth.

CHAPTER 11

I OUTLINED OUR STRATEGY as I drove: first the school to get any information we could on Alice, then the I.R.S. office in Sweetbay to see what we could find on Harley. I suspected I was going to have to push Mary Alice on the house search if that was ever going to happen. She seemed to have fallen back into her brooding mood, staring at her hands in her lap as she pushed at the cuticles, one by one.

After maybe fifteen minutes of silence she said, not lifting her head, "You know what my mother said to me once?"

It was a rhetorical question, so I waited for the answer.

"I was eleven, I think, but kind of . . . developed already. We were in the upstairs bathroom. I'd just got my period and she was showing me about pads and things. And then she just started staring at me. For a long time. Or it seemed long to me: I started thinking I must have done something wrong again. Like maybe the blood was my fault. But then she said, 'It's lucky that you're plain. The boys won't be after you all the time, tempting you to sin.'"

I glanced at her, but she was facing straight ahead,

those startling blue eyes inert, as though seeing more of the past than the present. I let some silence go by before I asked, "Does she talk about sin much?"

"We're Catholic," Mary Alice said, as though that answered the question. From my jaundiced Protestant perspective, it pretty much did.

"I've been thinking about Mother a lot since this whole thing started. You think she doesn't treat me too well, don't you?"

I took my right hand from the wheel long enough to make a hold-it gesture with my palm. "I've been with the woman for only two hours," I said. "Less. And it doesn't matter what I think anyway. It's your relationship; you've got to assess it for yourself."

"I know." Mary Alice was quiet for several moments, then said, "I know she treats me like a child. And not a very bright child either."

I glanced at her again, but she was talking mostly to herself now. "She's so beautiful, and so smart, I guess I never thought I could compete with her."

Compete? I thought. For what? The old Oedipal thing? I opened my mouth to give her some pearl of my wisdom when suddenly she brightened and turned to me. "That's what we can do!" she said. "Mother will be gone to church Sunday morning. We can search the house then."

We? I thought.

She seemed to pick up on the hesitation. "You will come with me, won't you?" she said, her anxiety strange, I thought, since it was her own home we were talking about. It wouldn't exactly be breaking and entering.

"Don't you go to church too?" I asked, stalling for time. I'd promised Gray the whole weekend.

"Of course," she said. Then with a sly smile, "But maybe this Sunday I could be sick."

I grinned. "No 'personal days' from Mom?"

She returned the smile, but with the rueful twist that lifted her mouth on one side only.

"Do you have any idea where she keeps legal papers?" I asked. "Any safe or anything in the house?"

"There's a safe behind that Madonna painting in the living room. But I've seen her open it and there's only her jewelry in there. The good things of her mother's."

"No papers at all? Marriage? Divorce? Death?"

"Not that I ever saw."

"Who else knows the combination?"

"Uncle Wendell does. I've heard her tell him to go in and get her some piece of jewelry, when she used to dress up and go out a lot."

"How about your birth certificate? Have you ever seen that?"

"No," she said. Then with a guilty expression, "I did look for it once. In my mother's dresser drawers. But I didn't find it."

"Did you look for it anywhere else in her room?"

"No!" she said. "I'm not even supposed to go in her room."

"How old were you then?" I asked, wondering at what age she'd decided she didn't belong to her family. Although maybe we all hit that point. My own parents had been more than ten years past the usual bearing age when I came along. There was a time I had sought that kind of legal confirmation.

"Eleven."

There are two groups of schools on the island: One on the west side, just south of Sweetbay, called the

Prince Island United School System, and one on the east side ten miles north of Port Angelina, formed a decade later and called the Eastern Island Educational Complex. Each has an elementary, a middle school, and a high school. Formed by the union of a scattering of local schools, the clusters were conceived by worried educators in the early seventies who looked at such mergers as a way to save money and manpower, while incidentally solving any incipient "diversity mandates," as the superintendent at the time called them. In other words, the threat of integration. Though the greater part of the island was and still is pretty homogeneous toward the pale-complected end of the color spectrum, the naval base has a more checkered racial mix. Those nightly images on the TV of federal troops at schoolhouse doors were very motivational for Prince Island bureaucrats to find ways to head the integrators off at the pass. The island taxpayers, each and every one, now share funding 50–50 with the Navy for the base's school system—as a separate entity.

The EIEC as a whole occupies eight acres of what used to be farmland, its mass somewhat forbidding after the sylvan drive down Wolf Road from #309, then west on Applejack, where a rash of new clone single-family housing, carved from the northern tip of Shepherd's Woods, hints of incursions to come.

Still, nothing quite prepares you for the sweep of brick and concrete that looms out of the alfalfa fields after you cross the bridge over Whisper Creek and hang a dead-end left onto Trident.

At least a third of the acreage is in parking. And more than another third is devoted to playing fields for every sport known to child, from the elaborate steel-pipe jungle gyms in primary colors that wrap two sides of Unit One at its eastern end, to the imposing Simpson Stadium that towers over Unit Three to the west.

The school buildings themselves, of brick the color of well-trod sand, are all one-story assemblages of rectangles set at odd angles, like multiple choices on a geometry quiz. Lined by tailored hedges, with a token Japanese maple here and there, the units are barely within sight of each other, the maze of blacktop walkways connecting each only to its parking lot and fields of play. Togetherness in educational cooperatives, it would appear, can go only so far.

Mary Alice had attended the EIEC herself, all three levels. And though she'd have entered the first grade only after her sister had apparently been deported, it was this middle school that Alice most likely would have been attending at the time. My client's assignment was to find out if any helpful information lay concealed in her sister's records, including a forwarding address. My experience with the school system had convinced me that one relative was worth a thousand lies when it came to squeezing confidential information from the educational bureaucracy.

Mary Alice started tensing up the minute we rolled onto the freshly graveled parking lot of the middle school; and by the time we had locked the car and were heading for Unit Two, she had a grip on my arm that would have welded steel. Her school experience, I concluded, had not been altogether pleasant.

To be honest, I was having a few flashbacks myself. Virtually from the cradle, I'd had energy to burn that would likely have propelled me into real trouble at some point had my parents not been canny enough to recognize it early and enroll me at the age of five in the Southern Indiana Academy of Gymnastics Excellence. It took all my free time and then some, until at thirteen, shortly after I'd won the Midwestern Semifinals Competition, my hand slipped from the top uneven bar in practice, and my amateur career came to a crunching halt, fracturing my right foot in six places.

A steel pin was installed at Indianapolis General, whose pundits warned that if I didn't keep significant weight off the foot for the next several months, I could kiss an active life good-bye.

Enter the theater. At the time, the high school's Drama Club was casting a production of *The Glass Menagerie* and decided that my crutch made me a natural for the part of Laura. Later I learned that my mother, a pillar of the PTA, may have had something to do with the offer, but by then I was hooked. And I revised the image the next spring by landing the title role in *Lolita,* a stage adaptation being performed by the notorious Unmasked Players, a group dedicated to the overthrow of the complacency of our conservative town of Earl, Indiana. Not incidentally, it also put me in touch with my till-then suspended sexuality.

Now, as we pushed through the double doors of Unit Two, Mary Alice's fingernails still lodged securely in the flesh of my upper arm, we were met with another memory booster: that unmistakable odor of ripe sweat socks and fresh varnish that would send the most resistant adult back into his school years.

I'd never been in this unit before; my only contact had been with the high school, tracking a runaway's last days before leaving the island. Compared to that building's wealth of trophies in glass cases and murals by student artists, Unit Two was a real comedown. The floors were a relentless gray and the walls a gravel-textured pea green broken only by wide bands of color running along the walls at eye level, apparently as directional aids. At the first intersection a stripe of orange led to the right, cherry to the left, then choices of lime or sooty gold at the next juncture. Mary Alice moved like a sleepwalker but seemed to know where she was going, so we went right on orange, left on lime, then right again on royal blue. . . .

Mercifully, we seemed to have arrived while classes were in session, so there were only a few students wandering the halls, looking younger than I remembered being at their age. Lockers and numbered classroom doors lined the walls, until we came to a short white corridor after the blue one, at the end of which was a door that looked like real walnut, with OFFICE spelled in block white letters above it on the jamb.

Mary Alice paused and turned to look at me, then at my nod, opened the door.

The room inside was large, a good twenty by fifty feet, the layout unnervingly like that of a courtroom. The assemblage of desks on the right, each bearing a brass plaque that identified its function—BUILDING AND MAINTENANCE, COUNSELING, PERSONNEL, etc.—was separated from the aisle before us by two neat rows of straight-backed chairs, ten wide—to seat those waiting for service perhaps, though they smacked more of detention. None was occupied at the time, and the women at the desks beyond barely looked up from their work. By then I had formed an image of the administrators of this school as ex-army sergeants in three-piece suits who had chronic trouble moving their bowels.

To our left was a high, wide counter that ran the width of the room, bisected by a swinging gate. Inside and to the right of that path was a walnut door with a brass plaque announcing it as the principal's lair. To the left, a huge desk—not walnut, but not shabby either—was set at an angle to the corner that allowed its occupant to survey the entire room without turning her head.

It was this personage on whom Mary Alice's gaze had been fixed from the moment we passed through the door. And no wonder: The woman looked older than God and wore a level stare that said you were never too grown to be intimidated.

Gently, I detached my client's fingers from my arm, nodded to her, and stepped back to seat myself on one of the chairs, hoping I didn't look like a student awaiting her punishment.

Slowly, Mary Alice approached the counter and set her purse upon it, like a buffer between her and the old woman beyond, whose mass of wrinkles sagged from her brow to her jowls like the hide of a sea lion.

"Mary Alice," the woman said.

It was a statement, not a question. I did some quick math: Unless they'd had contact since, this woman had remembered that name for at least thirteen years.

Whether or not Mary Alice was surprised at this feat, I couldn't tell, positioned as I was behind her. But I began to question the wisdom of my insisting that Mary Alice, as a relative, be the one to make the request for information.

Her voice was steady, however, if soft, when she replied, "Mrs. Erskine."

"What may I do for you?" The words were warmer than the voice.

"I need some information," Mary Alice said, her volume dropping further as she added, "about my family."

The woman looked at her in silence for a moment before she asked, "Who in your family?"

"My sister."

Slowly, the woman rose, a black shawl falling from her head and shoulders to the back of the chair, revealing a frail body scarcely taller than my own.

Without the shawl over her head the woman was totally bald, and as she hobbled to the counter I could see that her eyes were clouded with cataracts that substantially lessened the force of her gaze. When she arrived, she regarded Mary Alice without expression for several moments, then said, "Alice."

"Yes." The word was barely above a whisper. "You remember her?"

"Who of us could forget her?" Mrs. Erskine said, her voice brisk now, all business. "We didn't have her long at least, that was a mercy."

The harshness of her words seemed not to be directed at Mary Alice. And there was something about the stubborn jut of her jaw that made me suspect that the staff of this school had been given strict instructions—at least those still there when Mary Alice was about to enter among them—to hold their tongues on the subject of Alice Abbott.

"Do you know where she went?" Mary Alice asked. I could tell she was trying to keep her voice under control, adult to adult.

Mrs. Erskine squinted at her. "As I recall," she said slowly, "she went to live with her father. I believe that's what your mother said when she withdrew her files."

"You mean she has them? Everything about my sister?"

"I should think so," the woman said, her tone indicating that this was the end of the conversation.

"There isn't anything here? Copies or anything?"

"Paperwork?" she said, in a voice that seemed to

be revving up for a discourse. "All the paper in this place was thrown out when it went on the confounded computer. Like the machine was never going to forget a thing in its life and live forever. No power failures, no disk crashes, nothing. All that information just dumped in the garbage."

It was clear we wouldn't get any more information out of Mrs. Erskine today. I steered Mary Alice back through the multicolored maze.

It wasn't until we got back to the car that Mary Alice started trembling. An aftershock, apparently, of the encounter.

"You did great," I said, squeezing her wrist. "If you can get an ironclad lady like that to give up information, you can take on anybody."

She gave me a wan smile, then was silent as we pulled out of the parking lot and reversed our route. It wasn't until we were cruising down #309 headed west that she spoke.

"She remembered me," she said, a note of awe in her voice.

"Yes, she did." I glanced at her, but her face was blank.

"When I went there I thought she was the scariest person I'd ever met."

"I can see why."

"I guess Mother must have told everyone not to say anything about Alice."

I didn't answer, and she lapsed into silence again. It wasn't until we were passing the Redi-Clean that she seemed to recognize the scenery and turned in time to see its red-and-white building recede behind us.

"Where are we going?"

"You took the rest of the day off, right?" I said to her anxious expression.

"Yes, but—"

"We're going to pay a visit to the I.R.S. in Sweetbay. There are other ways we can try to get information on your father, but the I.R.S. probably has the most current. Unless he's stopped paying his taxes."

Her face had darkened again. "I don't know," she said slowly, "whether I want to see him or not." The tremor in her voice made me think the subject had been occupying much of her silence.

"You don't have to if you don't want to," I said. "Ever. That's my job. But if we're to get anything out of the I.R.S., you'll have to do the asking. They're real tight-lipped to anybody who's not a blood relative."

She nodded, though without enthusiasm. We spent the rest of the drive going over the scenario of how to plead our case. And I reminded her of tears: the last resort. My own wet baby-browns had wrung many an elusive bit of info from the hardest of hearts. But then, I probably looked more credible in the role of pitiful child than Mary Alice. Diminutiveness does have its advantages.

The island's tiny I.R.S. office is located in the federal/state/county building in the heart of Sweetbay's three-square-block downtown. It consists of one counter, one clerk, one computer, and no chairs. So I moved off to one side after we entered, posing as an innocent bystander while Mary Alice bravely bellied-up to the counter.

The clerk, a small middle-aged Hispanic woman, was tending to her coiffeur at a mirror set upon one of the low gray file cabinets in an alcove off to our right. When she turned back she looked slightly surprised to see us, as though she didn't get much business. In late March, with filing time less than a month away, I had expected a handful, if not a line, of anxious citizens. Maybe they all used the 800 number at this point in the process. I'd just sent off my own paperwork to Howard Olk, the accountant recommended by my mentor Simon. I was new to this independent-contractor biz and didn't want to make any mistakes that could bring me under the scrutiny of everybody's favorite Big Brother.

The woman stepped up to the counter across from Mary Alice and said briskly, "Yes?"

She was wearing a red sweater dress that clung to her compact curves. Her short-cropped black hair was permed and now perfectly combed. Gold-rimmed glasses hung from a gold chain, like a necklace, reaching to her ample bosom. Above her head on the back wall, a card identified her as Mrs. Anita Thomas, and I wondered idly whether she had married a gringo named Thomas or changed Tomas to a more American spelling. Below her ID hung a stack of numbers, black-on-white plastic squares, that seemed to indicate Mary Alice was Number 19.

"I need to find my father," Mary Alice said to the woman, her voice already throbbing with emotion.

All right, I thought—go, girl!

"This is the I.R.S.," the woman said, her tone as flat as her gaze.

Mary Alice started to turn toward me, then checked herself. "I know it is," she said, "but I hoped you might help." She took a breath, then the words came in a rush. "My mother's very ill, you see, and she wants to see him again before she dies." Her voice broke on the word *dies* and she stopped. Tears were welling in her eyes and a few spilled over. "I don't know what I'll do if she dies," she said. "I was almost three when he left and now—" The tears were coming faster. "Now I hear I have a sister, but she must be with him and I don't know where to look, not for anybody." And the sobbing started in earnest.

Mrs. Thomas looked alarmed, as I was a bit myself. Mary Alice's state of distress was clearly above and beyond the call of our scenario. I moved to her side and put a hand on the small of her back. Mrs. Thomas looked at me, clearly hoping I could help.

"I'm Mary Alice's cousin," I said to her. "I'm sorry. This is a very hard time for her."

"What's his name, the father?" she asked me.

I turned to let Mary Alice take the question if she could.

Her sobbing had subsided a little, and she tried to get her breathing under control. "Harley Abbott," she said with a little gasp.

The woman moved to her computer, lifted her glasses to her eyes, and hit keys until the screen suited her. "Spell it," she said, and my client did.

"*L-E-Y*?"

"Yes."

"Abbott, two *B*s, two *T*s?"

"Yes," Mary Alice said.

"Middle name?"

"I don't know. Maybe he didn't have one."

Mrs. Thomas sent us a look to let us know that the answer had not pleased her, then set to punching the keys again. She frowned at one screen after another.

"You sure your father is on this island?"

"No. No, I don't think he is. Though I guess he could be and I never knew."

"What about the county?"

"I don't know."

"The state?"

"I just don't know, I'm sorry."

"So many Abbotts . . ." she muttered.

"Could we start with the narrowest search and expand it as we need to?" I suggested.

Mrs. Thomas looked at me for a moment, then came back to the counter. "You got any ID?" she said to Mary Alice.

My client seemed relieved there was a question she could answer. She set her bag on the counter and unzipped the front flap on three sides so that it lay level toward her. There was a checkbook in a little pouch and four credit cards in individual pockets across from it, separated by three Bic stick pens, each in its own little loop. On the facing side were a five-by-eight pad of lined white paper and a booklet marked ADDRESSES, both held by their cardboard backing in their own slots in the beige vinyl. Mary Alice removed the top card—a driver's license—and handed it to the clerk, who studied it so long I thought she might be memorizing it.

At last she said, "You got anything else?"

Mary Alice quickly pulled the next card and handed it to her. It looked to be a Sears credit card.

The woman glanced at it, then handed them both back. "What's your social-security number?"

Mary Alice recited it.

"What's his?"

An uncharacteristic note of exasperation crept into Mary Alice's voice as she said in measured phrases, "I don't know. I was hoping you could help me find that out."

She stole a glance at me then, perhaps to see whether that slight edge in her tone had been an error on her part. I gave her the most imperceptible of nods, and she turned her gaze back to the woman, who looked from one to the other of us again, then returned to her computer.

She hit keys in silence for a while, making occasional notes on a pad to the left of the keyboard. Finally, she gave a shrug and printed out the screen, bringing the printout back to where we were standing.

"Okay," she said, "here's what I got." She held up the pad as though proving her sources. "Two hundred fifty-seven Abbotts in state of Washington, two *B*s, two *T*s. Twenty-four H. Abbotts, two is Harley."

"Two?!" Mary Alice shot me an excited glance.

"Not here," Mrs. Thomas went on. "One Spokane, one Seattle. Sixty-one Abbotts in Seattle, two *H*s, one Harley."

"Do you have addresses for the two Harleys?" I asked. "And when they last filed?"

Mrs. Thomas lifted her chin to peer at me through the bifocal squares at the bottom of her glasses. "Is all here," she said, in a tone that did not invite further questions.

Mary Alice must have thanked her four times before I got her out the door. Back in the car she said, "That's good, isn't it? Two Harley Abbotts?"

"It's a start," I said cautiously, squinting at the notes on the printout in Mrs. Thomas's tiny hand. Two in the entire state of Washington was not great odds. And the one in Seattle hadn't filed since '79.

"What do we do next?" she said.

"I start making some calls and checking some addresses," I said. "I'll be in Emerald tomorrow; I'll see what I can do from there."

"But you'll be back Sunday, won't you?" she said, the anxiety back in her voice. "To go through Mother's things with me?"

This was beginning to feel like baby-sitting. On the other hand, it was likely that the chances of finding valuable information would be improved by my participation. "Okay, I guess I can get back by then. You said eleven?"

"She usually leaves about ten-thirty. She likes to socialize before the service. And after."

"I'll be there by ten forty-five. I'll park down the street and watch the house before I come. What signal do you want to give me to let me know she's gone?"

Mary Alice's face lit up like a child's at Halloween. "Oh!" she said. "A signal!"

"What windows face the front of the house?"

"The ones in the living room. And the dining room . . . I know: I'll release a drape on the dining room window. Just one side, so it'll look different, once she's gone."

"Perfect."

CHAPTER 12

I DROPPED MY CLIENT AT HER CAR, then doubled back to the school complex. I sympathized with Mary Alice's troubles, but I'd had all I could take of her fragility for one day. I wanted to try another source at the schools to see if I could get a look at this elusive sister. It always helps to see the object of your investigation, and I didn't want to wait for Sunday's search of the house in the hope of finding Alice in some family photo tucked away from Mary Alice's inquiring eyes.

It was four twenty-five, but the doors to Unit Two were still unlocked, and I entered to empty hallways. I'd caught sight of a room I wanted to explore further, so I moved on silent sneakers, right on orange, left on lime, then left again on scarlet, toward a door marked LIBRARY.

The door was ajar, and while I had no reason to believe that my request would be denied, I was glad to find the room beyond it empty. If I couldn't find what I was looking for, I could always pull out the old license and make my explanations then.

The books weren't hard to find. There were open shelves on three sides of the big rectangular room and wider shelves down the center, set on cabinets with closed doors. After a quick scan of the shelves revealed nothing of that distinctive shape, I began opening cabinets. In the second range I found them: row after row of yearbooks in various colors, with gold numbers on the spines to designate the year. Many of the older books were missing, pilfered by nostalgic—or vengeful—grads perhaps. That included several in the range of years I was looking for, but I got lucky with my fourth book. In Carolyn Sanderson's seventh-grade class, I spotted her with a little shock of recognition, as though she were looking straight at me with that expressionless stare. The family resemblance was there, but she looked as distanced from any family embrace as she did from the rest of her class.

You noticed the hair first: bright red, short as a boy's, and clearly not her natural color. And there were those same intense blue eyes. Neither invited intimacy. Still, there was something touching, vulnerable about the girl. Perhaps it was the delicacy of her features, so like her mother's, the fragile bones of her face and a mouth that still looked soft even though the lips were pressed firmly together, as though to stop all conversation before it could start.

I glanced around quickly, still saw no one, and tore the page carefully from the volume, leaving a ragged edge nonetheless.

I checked the next year, and the next. No sign of her. Truancy or absence, as Mrs. Erskine had implied?

Then I backtracked my route and headed for Unit One of the system. I wanted to see how this girl had looked earlier in her life.

Unit One looked no kin to Unit Two. The walls were full of the bright artwork of children, from small handprints of preschoolers to more sophisticated drawings of family groupings before family houses. Everywhere they radiated hope.

I had to ask directions to the library from a building-maintenance man whose name below his title identified him as Floyd. He steered me down another couple of halls, past a cafeteria smelling of sloppy joes and chocolate pudding, to a room with windows on two sides and small square tables with chairs in primary colors.

The young woman inside, probably a high-school student, looked to be preparing to leave, shelving the last books from a cart, her coat and backpack lying next to them. I identified myself and told her what I was looking for and the dates of the likely yearbooks. "I can see you're getting ready to close," I said, "but I'd appreciate taking a quick look if I could."

"Sure, no problem," she said, and led me to the appropriate shelves. "You're really a private eye?" she said as I took the first volume from the shelf. 'Wow.'

I grinned. "Some days are more "wow" than others."

"Are you on a case?" she said, her green eyes wide and bright.

She caught my hesitation and hurried to say, "But you probably can't talk about it, right? It's, like, confidential."

I agreed, and she reluctantly backed off to let me look in privacy.

I started with the year Alice would have been in fifth grade and worked backward. I found her in none of the class pictures for grades five through three and was about to conclude that Alice Abbott must have gone to elementary school elsewhere when I saw the face in the second-grade class of one Mrs. Virginia

Farkas. Alice was on the end of the second row of children, one thin arm bent in a sling.

Her expression here was anything but defiant. A mixture of fear and sadness dimmed the bright blue eyes, and I leaned to look closer at the right side of her face, which seemed to be in shadow, though no one else's was. I checked the first-grade classes of the year before but didn't find her, leaving me to wonder whether Alice Abbott failed to show on most school-picture days for a reason.

The look in the girl's eyes haunted me on the drive home, and by the time I pulled alongside Free's muddy pickup, I wanted only to curl up under my comforter, surrounded by the fragrant whispering pines, and let sleep leave the often-ugly world of humans behind.

Free was on her hands and knees in the garden, planting snow peas in little hillocks beneath a row of strings dangling from a line above. Only days after planting, she'd told me when she brought the packet home, the hard seeds would crack and the shoots would reach out to grasp the strings and coil upward.

"I'm going to bed," I said, gesturing with my head toward the camper.

She lifted her arm to consult her shockproof, waterproof, damageproof watch and informed me that it was only 6:17. "Your head giving you trouble?" she asked.

"Not really."

"Well then, why don't you finish plantin' these peas and I'll go in and tend to dinner? I got some greens 'n' ham cookin'. I'll just do the corn bread and we can eat before you lay your stomach down."

Free got into soul cooking, like soul speech, when she was in a nurturing mood. I saw her tactic but was too tired to resist.

I took the packet and knelt, indifferent to the threat of stains to my best jeans. And one by one I nosed the little seeds into the soil, four to a hill, aiming each little mound at a string.

Soon the repetition began to feel like a mantra, a physical chant of trust in the life force. All around me, plants were breaking dormancy. One row over, the first bright curls of lettuce were parting the rich mix of topsoil and compost Free'd been preparing all winter. And in the next, the darker sprouts of spinach seemed to promise a season of health and enrichment.

The veggies were only the second coming though. Just as Free had spent the last year single-handedly transforming her simple hunter's cabin into a cottage worthy of the (upscale) English countryside, she had been doing the same for the landscape. Old and new English roses with names like Peach Blossom and Dapple Dawn were set into specially prepared soil lining the flagstones of the front walk, along with fragrant heathers and the soft dusky pink of hellebores, the Lenten rose. At the corners of the cottage, spotted among the boxwoods, clusters of white candytuft and airy lemon sprays of leopard's bane shone like rays of light against the dark green.

Even in this kitchen garden, running along the back porch to the outdoor shower I use most mornings and evenings, interplantings of flowers bloomed. Species of red tulips and the first petals of golden forsythia glowed in the late-afternoon sun.

It was the tulips that recalled to me the bright red hair of the young Alice in what was probably the last photograph of her school years. That was what had sent Mary Alice bolting from the car to pursue the young woman at the post office. She was beginning to remember.

My first impulse was to share that news with her immediately. But then I remembered the hard lessons learned in my own rape-survival group: The psyche has good reason to remember what it remembers only when it's ready.

In the morning I caught the seven-thirty ferry, hoping to pack a whole weekend into one day with Gray. In a way, it would be easier, for I find the first day in Emerald to be a relatively uncomplicated pleasure full of long talks, long walks, and fabulous sex. Sundays, though, often find me in a weakened condition, and I catch myself thinking how nice yellow gingham curtains would look in the kitchen and how that ratty sweater Gray always wears deserves to be replaced by a nice heather tweed to match his eyes. And I won't even mention how babies spring to my sight everywhere we go.

The day was glorious, the first that spring that felt as though winter was really over. We bicycled into the hills above Century Bay and lay in the sun, talking and not talking. When the light began to fade, we coasted back into town and stuffed ourselves with pizza, then with each other.

We were both in a deep and peaceful sleep when the call came, and I was barely listening until Gray's hushed voice said, ". . . totally burned?" and I was wide awake.

"I'll be right there," he said, but I was already out of bed before him, pulling on my jeans.

He frowned. "No. Not this time."

"Where is it?" I said.

"Gateway Park, at the shelter."

Immediately I pictured the great stone fireplaces at

either end of the long roofed picnic shelter and shuddered in spite of myself.

"This is something you do not need to see. Again," he said.

I glanced at him with a raised eyebrow.

"Okay, don't tell you what you need," he said, somewhat sarcastically.

I waited till my head cleared the sweatshirt I was pulling over it to say, "Sweetheart, I appreciate the concern. But the man meant to kill me. I take that personally. I'm already involved."

As we rushed through the rest of our dressing and headed for the car, I went over it out loud. "They've never been this close together before. And he's all over the lot—Seattle, the island, now here. What do you think?"

"Whatever's driving him is escalating. And the M.O. has started to vary. I *hope* that means he'll start making mistakes."

"What's it been? One every other month, then none for six, now two in succession? How old is this one?"

"They don't know yet. The body's pretty badly burned."

When we'd bumbled through the garage clutter to the car, Gray slammed the bubble on top and we took off under the unnerving sound of the siren, through streets that were almost deserted, as though people had known to stay under their own roofs that night.

The noise precluded conversation, but the images kept running through my head: the sight of that burning pyre, the smell of gasoline and cooked flesh. I wondered if Gray knew how much, in fact, I did *not* want to see—and smell—that sight again. But it's odd how once you've made such horrors your business, the questions of comfort and personal choice virtually cease to exist. It's your job, so you do it. And while this was not my case, strictly speaking, it was now definitely my business.

The parking lot nearest the shelter was packed with emergency vehicles—squad cars, sheriff's blue-and-whites, two fire trucks—even an ambulance, though it was obvious from the first glance that it was too late for medical care.

There was no pyre; the body was on the ground, slumped against a crude wooden cross, its upright post driven into the soft ground just outside the shelter, and there was a knife sticking out of the woman's chest. The dry firewood stacked in the shelter for the use of picnickers had been piled around the body, so there was little left by the time the fire had been put out.

"We left it till you got here, Chief," a young uniformed officer named Curtis said to Gray, falling into step with him as we approached the scene. "Everybody kept back, except the fire people."

"The M.E. here?"

"He's on his way."

"Are there clothes? Any ID at all?"

"None we could find. Even the hair's burned."

"No prints."

"That's the strange thing," Curtis said. "There hasn't seemed to be any particular attempt to burn the fingers like there's been before. Prints on the feet are gone, but it looks as though there's enough left of the fingers for at least one or two."

"From your mouth to God's ear," Gray said grimly.

He took over then, and I circled the body at a careful distance. It would not be moved until the medical examiner arrived and did his initial assessments.

I made my own guess, though, about the lack of burns on the fingers. In the earlier strikes of the Crucifixer, when the dead woman's body was laid on a pyre, the hands were arranged folded on the chest, with the crucifix tucked into them. But this victim's body seemed to have been upright when it burned. From the position of the corpse, she could have been bound with her arms over the horizontal post of the cross and her hands behind her back, held by bonds now largely burned away. There was some ancient, evil aspect to the scene, as though this body was less an offering to God than to the devil. The chill air suddenly turned colder.

Like the others, this act reeked of premeditation. No woman was likely to have been walking in the park alone at this time of night, to be seized by a crazed killer in a moment of impulse. The victim must have been found elsewhere and either killed there or brought live to this chosen spot. I hoped it was the former; the thought of any conscious person being bound and gagged and hauled away, to watch while her cross was being made, knowing what was coming. . . .

It made me literally sick with horror, and I backed away. I took deep breaths of the night air; I couldn't get enough of it. Above, a nearly full moon shone bright in a sky of midnight blue. I leaned against a tree trunk, gazing upward, then slowly lowered my sight again to the body.

The knife. Why the knife? It couldn't have penetrated far enough to serve as anchor to the cross. But it must have been driven with deliberate force to be still lodged there following the fire.

I began to move slowly back and forth, studying the ground between my position and the body. I found one, then two of the sort of thing I was looking for: pieces of wood a couple of feet long that looked to have been whittled to a point, then pounded against some impenetrable object.

I picked them up with tissues from my jeans pockets, carried them over to where Gray was just rising with the M.E. from his examination of the body, and waited while he gave orders for cordoning off the crime scene and the removal of the corpse.

He turned then and saw what I was holding.

"Stakes?" I said. "Through the heart? The way to kill a witch?"

He turned my wrists back and forth, examining the wood.

"The victim on the island had a nail driven into her chest," I said. "Maybe all he had at the time. This time maybe he brought a knife, but the wood was still too soft to penetrate."

Gray nodded, staring at them, then the body. "Where were they?"

"About throwing distance," I said. "As if the killer got frustrated and flung them away."

Gray bent and picked up two plastic evidence bags and held them open for me to deposit a stake in each.

Then he looked at me for a moment. "Let's go home," he said. "There's not much more we can do here in the dark."

I noticed the *we*.

He deposited the bags with the rest of their kind. "I'll come back in the morning," he said. Then, with a shadow of his adorable lopsided grin, "Since you're deserting me, at least I'll have something to occupy my time."

"Thoughtful of the monster," I said.

Gray spoke to two of his men, then put his arm

around my shoulders as we trudged back to the car and dropped wearily into its bucket seats.

We were silent for the first ten minutes of the drive home, while scenes of the killings flashed before my mind's eye like stage sets on a turntable. Crucifixes, crosses, fire: all Christian icons. Was he trying to cleanse or destroy? Or both? Was he playing God? Getting back at God? Striking a bargain? I recalled the image of Abraham preparing to make a burnt offering of his son—a scene out of an early illustrated Sunday school text.

But it wasn't a simple equation. Hate, shame, rage, obsession—they all seemed wound up together in his acts. "Salem all over again," I said, voicing the thought. "Exorcising the power of women."

Gray drove for some minutes more in silence before he said, "Gotta hand it to you, Ms. Piper. Despite my best efforts to the contrary, you seem to have made quite a detective of yourself."

"Damn straight," I said, and grinned into the darkness.

CHAPTER 13

I DROVE PAST MARY ALICE'S HOUSE FIRST, saw the left side of the dining room drapes already down, and parked a block away, around the corner on Moss.

I felt a bit hung over from the events of the night before, my head a jumble of conflicting priorities. One sister missing; five women murdered. But for Mary Alice, the choice was clear, and she was my client. Besides, what help could I really be in the search for the Crucifixer? There were now legions of detectives on that case, and Mary Alice had only me. So I tried to put that part of my brain on hold and rally my forces for my client.

Mary Alice opened the door before I reached it, fairly sizzling with excitement. "She's gone," she whispered, apparently unaware that her whispering contradicted the statement.

"Let's go," I said, gesturing for her to precede me up the staircase.

The upper hallway was narrow, leading to a doorway at each end. Mary Alice gestured to the right. "My room," she whispered, and moved to the left. "Mother's room," she said, in a more dramatic whisper.

But I wanted to get a sense of the whole floor first and turned right toward what seemed to be another, perpendicular hallway about eight feet down.

"It's here," Mary Alice called in a stage whisper, her hand still on the knob of the other door.

But when I didn't join her, she came up behind me.

"Where does this lead?" I asked.

"I don't know. That part's been closed off," she said. "We don't need it, and Mother says it wastes heat if it's left open."

"Was Alice's bedroom in that part?" I asked, moving to the door at the end of the short hall. It was locked.

"I guess." Mary Alice's voice was strained. "I don't think we should disturb it."

If she was more willing to "disturb" her mother's room, I guessed the inviolability of the rooms beyond that door must have been impressed upon her early and firmly.

"Are there any other bedrooms in the house?" I asked.

"Not really. There's a sort of den downstairs with a Hide-a-Bed my uncle uses when he stays over, but these two are the only real bedrooms."

I stared at the door, trying to visualize how much space lay beyond it based on the downstairs floor, until Mary Alice said nervously, "We don't have much time."

"Right," I said, and we backtracked to Shirleen's room, where Mary Alice paused to listen at the door as though to hear if her mother were inside, even though she'd just seen her leave. A potent presence, this woman, I thought, even in her absence.

My digital watch said 11:12.

The room the door opened to was large, with tall

windows along the facing wall, their only covering white veils, with a ruffled peach valance at the top. Peach-and-white was the color scheme for most of the room, both walls and woodwork painted white, with more peach ruffles skirting the dressing table and the bed, which dominated the room. A queen-size cherry four-poster with ornately carved newels, the bed was draped with gauzy white swags that all but concealed the pale peach comforter and eyelet pillowcases within. I motioned Mary Alice to the other side of the bed, and we lifted the mattress to confirm that there was nothing hidden between mattress and box spring. A look under the dust ruffle revealed nothing on the floor either.

Twin dressers made an *L* in the northeast corner of the room, and the entire west wall was occupied by a wardrobe, shuttered by three bifold doors. A tripart mirror stood positioned at the far end, before a large full-length mirror on the wall, affording a 360-degree view of oneself—to avoid any horrors, I supposed, such as an upturned label showing at the neck or a glimpse of slip below the hemline.

To the right of the bed, Shirleen's dressing table was kidney-shape, nearly surrounding the velvet-covered stool, and lit by the professional round bulbs at the top used in theater dressing rooms. On either side were the tools of her trade, hung on white hooks: hair dryer, curling iron, steam gun to remove any lingering wrinkles from one's skirt. At the right on the tabletop was a silver-backed comb-and-brush set, along with one of those rat-tailed combs that tend to the finer parts of the hairdo, while on the left were enough jars of face cream, eye-shadow packs, and mascara tubes to make up the entire cast of *Cats*.

Above, on either side of the mirror, were little

shelves holding lipsticks—more than twenty by my quick count—arranged by color from faint pink through reds to irridescent bronzes; and perfume bottles perched like debutantes, holding tinted fragrances within their bouffant skirts.

I looked around. The whole room was so ultrafeminine, it was hard to imagine a man ever sharing it. Maybe Shirleen had redecorated after her husband left, though I suspected the woman would see to it that her environs were always to her taste, as complimentary as her hair color or her wardrobe.

I assigned Mary Alice one dresser and I took the other, feeling carefully among the undies and the sweaters for anything that felt unwearable. When neither dresser proved fruitful, I had her hold each drawer while I felt along its perimeter and underside, favored hiding places of the secretive set. But they were clean.

I glanced at my watch: 11:20. I was itching to see what lay beyond the doors of the closet, so I sent Mary Alice into the bathroom to check any possible hiding places there, such as within or behind the toilet tank and any space behind the medicine chest. I'd never heard of anything but drugs being stashed in such places but thought we should leave no enclosure unprobed.

I began my search of the wardrobe by opening all three bifold doors to see the full range of its contents. Even I was amazed. I've seen some lavish racks of costumes backstage, but the expanse of clothing in that layout was truly excessive. From the furs on the left, hung in heavy plastic zipper bags, to the scarves hanging from a revolving rack at the right end, Shirleen had awaiting her the perfect ensemble for any occasion. Two shelves on the floor housed shoes—the upper for dress, lower for casual shoes, if the term was even appropriate to Shirleen's style. In between was everything from ball gowns to designer jeans.

But my interest was most drawn to the top shelf and the multitude of hatboxes stacked there. I dragged over the dressing-table stool and began my search, shuffling the stacks to open one box, then another, and running my hand along the insides of both box and hat. Even these Shirleen had apparently arranged in order, from pillboxes and berets on the left to a progressively large and ornate collection as I moved right. The woman's unvaryingly good taste prevailed over all though: high style without flash, never to command more attention to the worn than the wearer.

Mary Alice returned to pronounce the bathroom unproductive just as I was trying a hat on for size: a little black velvet number that was sewn slouched over the right eyebrow. She gave a little gasp, though whether at the effrontery of my trying on her mother's hat or at the fetching sight of me wearing it, I did not ask myself.

"Mother used to collect hats," Mary Alice said.

"She doesn't anymore?" I teetered on the stool, leaning to peek at my image in the mirror centrally located on that shelf.

"Not really. Just a veil to church. She says God doesn't like a lot of show."

"She's very religious then?"

"The last year or so she has been. Very."

I noticed a large prescription bottle in Mary Alice's hand and asked about it.

"Just my nerve pills," she said. "I take them to sleep. Mother gets them from her doctor, and I'm almost out."

"You don't take them every night, do you?"

"Oh, yes, for as long as I can remember. Mother says I'm high-strung."

I put the hat I was wearing back in its box and opened the one next to it, lifting gold tissue to reveal a wide yellow straw-and-chiffon creation, which I lifted carefully to discover beneath its curving brim a fat stack of envelopes.

"You recognize these?" I asked, lifting out one of the packets.

"I don't think so," Mary Alice said. "What are they?"

I was opening the top envelope as she spoke, and I pulled out the contents: photographs. From my perch on the stool, my hands were at the level of Mary Alice's head, and she rose on tiptoe to see better.

The first photo was black and white, of a man and a woman standing in front of this house, though it looked brand-new and the shrubbery was small enough to have come in gallon pots. The man held a little girl, about one, and all three were smiling brightly at the camera.

The next several photographs were of the same three—beside a Christmas tree, on a carousel, before the monkey cage at a zoo. The little girl was a toddler in the pictures and looked very much like the woman, who looked very much like Shirleen did now. There was also a middle-aged woman dressed in a white uniform in a few of the pictures—the nanny, I guessed, who was probably the photographer in the others. There was no sign of a son.

In the next packet, in which Shirleen looked to be about three, an infant appeared, held in the mother's arms. The smile on the woman's face was still dazzling, though the man I assumed to be the father appeared more sober. "Your uncle's the younger," I said to

Mary Alice. I'd almost forgotten he wasn't the elder of the two, which he certainly looked to be.

In subsequent packets, both children progressed in age in the photos, until Shirleen looked at least twelve and the boy about nine, a gangly youth, though already taller, like his father, than the women in the picture.

The next packet was much slimmer, and there were no photos, only newspaper halftones with the captions cut off, picturing the nanny and the two children at a funeral. All three looked stunned, standing in the shelter of a black umbrella before a grave site, alone except for a minister holding a Bible aloft like an offering.

"They both died," Mary Alice said. "She never says how, just that they died, leaving her and Uncle Wendell alone in the world. I think she was thirteen."

The next envelope seemed to contain wedding pictures and Shirleen was dressed in a white lace cocktail dress, standing before a stone chapel, a bouquet of spring flowers in her arms. The handsome young man beside her looked proud and a little smug, dressed in a white tuxedo with a wide scarlet cummerbund at his slim waist. But mostly they looked young.

Then there was the sound from downstairs of the front door opening, and both of us froze. "It's Mother," Mary Alice whispered, aghast. My watch said only 11:42, and there'd been no sound of a car in the garage below, but even if it was the uncle, I had no desire to get caught poking about in family business.

"Go downstairs," I said to Mary Alice. "If it's your mother, stall her, get her to the back of the house so I can come down and get out the front door.

"Go!" I hissed before her limbs would move.

Quickly I tucked the photo I was holding into the

pocket of my jeans, put the rest of the envelopes back in the box with the hat over them, and got down from the stool. I scanned the contents of the closet for order before I closed the bifold doors as silently as possible and put the stool back in its place, ruffling the nap of its seat the wrong way with my hand to obliterate the prints of my sneakers. The way this woman organized her spaces, I suspected she'd notice anything that was not exactly as she'd left it.

I heard Mary Alice downstairs, talking a bit louder than she had to, I thought. Her mother's voice was quieter but had a plaintive tone to it I had not heard on my first visit. I went to the door to listen.

". . . got so bad I had to leave; Evelyn brought me. Oooh, I look forward to that service all week and seeing all the lovely people, God's people . . . Then this vicious migraine picks just this time to strike."

"Come back to the kitchen and I'll fix you some tea. You know how the chamomile helps when you get like this."

But the voice that answered was closer, sounding already on the stairs. "Bring it to me, would you? That's a dear. I have to lie down; this thing is blinding. And maybe a bowl of ice and a cloth for my forehead? It's the only thing that seems to help, that and prayer."

I was doing some praying myself as I looked wildly about the room for shelter. My gaze fell upon the dust ruffle on the bed and mentally measured its height against the thickest parts of my body. It would be close but worth a try.

I lifted the ruffle and lay flat on my back, sliding under the bed along the plush peach carpet. I had to hold my breath to clear the base of the frame above and for once was thankful that I was no bustier than I am. My last act was to run my hand along the carpet to obliterate any telltale signs of my presence before the door opened and Shirleen came, sighing, into the room.

The dust ruffle extended exactly to the carpet, so I had only sound to guide me as she crossed to her dressing table, presumably removed whatever she thought needed removing, then spread herself with a moan upon the bed, her body adding just enough weight to pin me to the floor.

Shirleen sighed and groaned while I gasped silently underneath, until Mary Alice arrived with the tea and ice. Then the bed sagged further while Shirleen sat up to sip the tea, as her daughter plumped the pillows behind her.

Mary Alice's voice was tight as she attended her mother, and I just hoped she wasn't looking about the room for me as nervously as her tone would indicate—although I knew Shirleen's usual self-absorption made it unlikely she would notice her daughter's behavior, however strange.

I was under there for hours, it seemed, though in fact it was probably more like twenty minutes, until Shirleen's migraine medication kicked in and I was able to unwedge myself to the sounds of her snoring and beat a quiet retreat. During that time, however, I found I'd fallen upon—or under—exactly what I was looking for.

The box spring of the bed rested not on wooden slats or a metal frame but on bands of heavy webbing that made a crossweave to hold the springs and mattress. And as I lay there with my nose wedged up against the weave, I saw at about chest level a manila legal-size envelope wedged between weave and springs.

At first it didn't quite register, as out-of-context as

it seemed. Then what was left of my breath caught, and I very slowly reached to touch it.

It would be the devil to remove, I realized, held so tightly in its web that it seemed to have merged with the strapping. And I had to wait until I was sure the woman was asleep before I even tried. It took about ten minutes, stopping when I heard the least sound of stirring from above, before I'd worked it out from between its clasping fabrics, leaving only a little of the envelope behind. And I waited even longer before I tried extricating myself.

The look of relief on Mary Alice's face when I came down the stairs was so comical, it was almost worth the close call. But I'd instinctively hidden the envelope under my shirt, tucked into the waistband of my jeans. Until I knew what was in it, I didn't want to excite—or alarm—my client unnecessarily.

As soon as I was out of sight of the house, I ran the rest of the way to my car before opening the envelope and easing its contents onto the passenger seat.

Right on top was Alice's birth certificate, issued by a hospital in Salt Lake City, Utah. The date of birth made her sixteen years older than Mary Alice's twenty-seven. Other than that, the information was minimal. *Name of Child* was listed only as *Alice; Name of Mother* was *Shirleen Holman;* and in the space for *Name of Father* was a single word: *Unknown*.

Mary Alice's was beneath it, from the Gabriel Clinic in Tyrone, Washington. It confirmed the birth date she'd given me and listed her parents as Shirleen and Harley Abbott.

Beneath that was a marriage license application issued in Sweetbay, between Shirleen Holman and Harley Abbott. The date was May of the same year as Mary Alice's birth in August.

I took the picture from my jeans pocket and smoothed the wrinkles out. Apparently, the empire cut of Shirleen's dress had been a practical necessity. But the bride didn't look all that much different from her present state of preservation. There was something eerie and uncomfortable about that, and I stuffed all the documents back in the manila envelope and took off for home to study them in the privacy of my woodland haven.

Free poked her head out her kitchen window when she heard me drive up. "Back from Paradise so fast?" she called.

"If you mean Emerald, I got back early this morning. I had a meeting with my client." Then I realized that without a TV and only a rare newspaper, Free might not know about the latest strike of the Crucifixer. I thought it might be best if she heard it from me, so I joined her in the kitchen.

When I'd finished the short version of the night before—and this morning, though I named no names—Free was not pleased.

"So after last night's little episode of restimulation, you come back here and go breaking and entering and hiding yourself under beds?" she said.

"It wasn't breaking and entering; it was my client's house."

"Tell that to the mother," she retorted. Then she sat down across from me. "Why can't you give yourself some kind of rest from all this? You look terrible, you know."

"Thanks a lot," I said.

"I mean it. You haven't even healed from your first encounter with this lowlife, and off you go chasing after him again. Then you come home and play burglar to unearth the tawdry little secrets of some wacko white folks."

I gave her a sharp look. "I didn't expect you of all people to be telling me to stay home with my knitting."

She looked at me intently, then held up both hands. "You're right. What business is it of mine? But I'm telling you anyway, girl: You don't have to play Superwoman every minute of your life. Take it from me. What happened back in those woods had to be terrifying, and I don't see you dealing with that fear. Or the anger. Any of that nasty stuff."

"Later for that," I said stubbornly. "I've got my own case to solve. Besides—" I stared at the fat glass bowl on the table, overflowing with the deep blue and white faces of pansies. "You know what they say about getting back on the horse."

"Yeah," Free retorted, "but you could try trotting before you gallop, you know."

I had to smile in spite of myself. She was probably right but you can't let your friends know that or you'll never hear the end of it. So I said only, with some dignity, "It is in my nature to gallop."

CHAPTER 14

BACK IN THE CAMPER, I spread the contents of the envelope on the bed and picked up Alice's birth certificate. There was something I'd missed. The data was printed on a pink background with rows of bunny heads that had all but obscured the line for *Age of Mother*. I peered closer: *13*.

Thirteen. That was Shirleen's age when her parents died, Mary Alice had said. I wondered whether the deaths or the pregnancy had come first. In any case, Harley Abbott could not have been Alice's biological father. Had he adopted her when he and Shirleen married? And Utah: What was she doing in Utah? I recalled the photo of the two children with the woman at a grave site in the rain and made a mental note to ask Mary Alice whether the grandparents had been buried locally and what, if anything, she knew about a Utah connection. I shuffled through the other documents, looking for a death certificate for the parents or adoption papers for Alice, but there was none.

I picked up the license application again. Shirleen's listed age could not be accurate. If she was thirteen when Alice was born, and Alice was sixteen when Mary Alice was born and they'd shipped her off,

Shirleen had to have been twenty-nine the year of her marriage and the birth. But the application listed her age as twenty-five—younger, though not as young as her new hubby, whose age was listed as twenty-three. Neither looked a day over eighteen. I wondered to what lengths Shirleen had gone to fake her age for the occasion. What lengths she went to now to look two decades younger than her apparent fifty-six.

I looked for a divorce certificate but found none. What I did find, though, was almost as interesting: certificates of registration for three high-tonnage trucks, which listed Harley Abbott as *Registered Owner*, but Shirleen Holman Abbott as *Legal Owner*. And they were dated two years *after* they'd supposedly separated, if Mary Alice was almost three.

They were clearly the originals. Like the pink color-washed background on Alice's birth certificate, the background on these was a faint green pattern of a continuous chain of coins bearing the bust of good old George, for whom the state is named.

I pulled out my pad and did some figuring. First Alice was expelled, then Harley, by the time Mary Alice was almost three. By the "jealous bitch," as Alice had called her mother in her letter. I wondered how early in the marriage Harley's attentions to his stepdaughter had begun and how soon Shirleen had become aware of them. Had they started when the husband entered the family, or had Alice maybe been the object of Harley's prurient interest from the beginning? To have been wed, as an older woman, just so the guy could get at her nubile daughter would have fried Shirleen's hide. Shipping them both off seemed almost a reasonable response, given the woman's vanity and self-centeredness. But then what was she doing buying trucks for the guy two years later?

I lay back on the bed to give my brain a rest. I'd seen no signs of forgiveness in Shirleen's attitude when her hubby's name came up at dinner. Maybe the transaction had been more one of business than pleasure. And control. What had she said? "The man's got nothing I haven't given him."

I raised the picture of the two of them into my horizontal range of vision. If he had married her for her money or her daughter, it was surely clear why she had married him. He was a handsome devil, with lots of curly black hair, classic Roman features, and a physique that would have sent Rodin running for the clay. Even allowing for the flattering lines of a tux, he was prime gigolo material. And though something about his confident smile suggested that he could not be altogether bought, it didn't seem to rule out being rented for profit. Definitely not your basic family man.

I closed my eyes. *Handsome devil.* What is there about a strikingly handsome man that makes the next word that pops into your mind *devil*? Do they have it too easy, and that in itself becomes corrupting? Our protestations to the contrary, it must be admitted that good guys often do finish last with women. Is it the danger, the lure of the destructive, if not the forbidden, that draws us to the "bad boys"?

I fell asleep on that thought, woke hours later, disoriented as I always am after a rare daytime nap.

The death of Shirleen's parents was still on my mind; if this had been any day but Sunday, I'd have gone straight to the *Grace Guardian* newspaper morgue to see if the obituary in the principal island paper could give me any new information on the next of kin. But Prince Island is still pure enough to close down most everything on Sundays. Even the Grace Library was closed for the day.

I sank my fingers into my hair and rubbed my scalp vigorously, being careful to detour around the lump. I needed a shower badly. But even more, I decided, I needed a run. The cotton batting in my brain, I was sure, had less to do with slugs to the head than with the lack of regular exercise.

So I changed to my running sweats and shoes and took off along my usual route. I didn't ask myself if I was really ready to revisit the scene of my downfall. I've found that often, things work out better if I just *do* it, without too much forethought.

And in fact, I felt no overwhelming trauma as I cleared the trees and the cabin's remains came into view. I stopped, then began jogging in place until I felt like pushing off to get nearer. The yellow crime-scene tapes still cordoned off the entire clearing, but evidence-gathering would have ended long ago, I knew, so I stooped under the tape and approached the makeshift pyre, scanning the ground as I went.

I was looking for stakes. The island victim had been stabbed in the chest with a nail, the officers said. But why a nail? Just because it was handy? According to the talk I'd heard the night before in Emerald, both that victim and this had been dead before the stabbing, strangled like the others. So what purpose had the stabbing served, and how significant was the instrument?

With my foot—just in case fingerprints might still matter—I poked at one after another of the charred fragments of board in the pile that had once been the pyre, moving them around and turning them over. From the shape it looked as though the mound had collapsed on itself once the body was removed, tossing off ashes and debris for several feet around it. So I searched in a widening circle.

The piece I found, about eight feet from the pile, was similar to the ones in Emerald, except that its point had been formed without the aid of a knife, apparently by breaking a board across the grain. But like the others, it had not proved strong enough to penetrate flesh, its point only blunted by the effort.

The implications were not heartening, I decided. Apparently the killer saw women—any women—as witches to be disempowered, requiring a stake through the heart. The fact that he hadn't brought a knife for the purpose suggested that this killing had been more impulsive than the others. But it had been repeated only days later elsewhere, with the same exorcistic gesture of the stake and the even more fiercely symbolic form of the cross. I wasn't sure what all that meant, but I knew I didn't like it.

I took off my headband and used it to pick up the failed stake. So burdened, I turned and headed toward home, feeling like Red Riding Hood running through the woods of The Wolf. And yes, with some of that anger Free had mentioned, at having my own neighborhood now feel unsafe for a simple run.

CHAPTER 15

BY THE NEXT MORNING, I was wishing I were quintuplets. There were at least five different directions I wanted to go in at once. Besides the newspaper morgue for information on the death of Shirleen's parents, I wanted to check the city and county offices for things like divorce decrees, traffic tickets, vehicle and business licenses, and to pin down my client for more hard facts than she had yet come up with. Not to mention my continuing curiosity about the Crucifixer case, which made me itch to go over the Prince Island, Emerald, and Seattle police reports to see if they'd come up with anything I hadn't heard yet.

But it was no contest: My immediate objective had to be the locating of Harley Abbott. He was the accused, and whatever the facts, I figured that if Alice had for some reason failed to make contact with her sister, her next move might very well have been to seek out the man she considered responsible for her trauma, past and present. In addition, even if he wasn't a current participant in the family, my bet was that he'd have a lot to tell about its members, and I could use all the information of that sort I could get.

Apparently, Shirleen had decided to throw both

Harley and Alice out at the same time, sending Alice off to her tormenter as vengeance for luring her husband away, as Shirleen would have seen it. Apparently, Alice's worst memories were of that period, when she'd had no family as buffer—if any of them had ever provided that. Wendell seemed about the only buffer Mary Alice had, but his relationship to the older daughter might have been much different.

I at least had a place to start looking. Two places: the old I.R.S. address and the address on the vehicle-registration certificates.

The latter lead was reinforced when, while sticking the purloined documents back in their ragged manila envelope, I felt a sliver of paper beneath the nail of my index finger and pulled them back out, felt in the envelope again, and retrieved a check. Dated two months after the registration certificates, the check was drawn on a Seattle bank and made out to Shirleen Abbott, by Harley Abbott, for four hundred and fifty dollars, for "lien payment." It was imprinted with the same address as the certificates and even had the bonus of a phone number—and yes, folks, that magic social-security number. Now, I thought, we were getting somewhere. Never mind that the check had been returned with the box marked by the bank for *Insufficient Funds;* two addresses were better than one, and I was off for Seattle.

First, though, I had to take my discovery at the murder site to the police. Out of loyalty, I'd make that the Grace police, and I could check my answering machine at the same time.

It felt good to be back in action, even if there were too few of me. I'd already laid out for myself more bases in Seattle than I could run in a day. So if I took Simon up on his offer and spent the night in Olympia, that would give me a second day in Seattle to pursue any unfinished business.

And it would be good to see a friendly face. Simon Ester Emmershaw is one of the few men I know who do not trigger my defenses—a necessary ingredient in a mentor. I can talk out cases with him, see if he spots anything I've missed. My compromise with Gray—you don't tell me your dangers, I won't tell you mine—pretty much rules out that sort of exchange between us. Besides, emotional ties muddy the mind. With Simon the mental airwaves are clear. And as a bonus he's got a computer system with data bases on-line for just about every electronic highway in the state and nation. Using such sources still feels like cheating to me; I guess I cling to the old gumshoe ethic of tracking down the bad guys using only shoe leather and the classic con. But if all else fails, there is the computer.

I called him from the office, and he assured me the welcome mat was still out. "How would lobster strike you for dinner?" he said in his Orson Welles voice. (Did I mention that Simon has old money, so sleuthing is more of a hobby for him than a meal ticket?)

"Strikes me in my favorite spot," I said, and told him I'd try to make it there by seven.

I then retired to the bathroom mirror and unwound my bandage. I'd decided I'd rather risk a reopened wound than be pegged as the "other victim" of the Crucifixer by everyone I needed to question. The dried blood the gauze was stuck to made the bandage nasty to remove, but at least it didn't release a fresh flowing, so I plopped my hat over the bump and went out to fight another day.

Downstairs, I dropped in on Gene Mulholland to ask him to keep an ear out for anything amiss he might hear from above while I was gone. I was still a bit uneasy about the sounds of the other night. Probably only paranoia, but still . . . I tried to soft-pedal my concerns to Gene, who tends to be a fussbudget himself, saying only that I'd be out of town for a couple of days and wanted to be sure things were secure. But it remained a strange request; there wasn't a lot of mayhem to be anticipated on Dahlia Street.

"Anything in particular going on?" he asked carefully.

Eugene Mulholland has the elongated body of a pole vaulter, the acuity of a card shark, and the caution of an accountant. They serve him well in his practice, which handles mostly corporate business, but if you want an impromptu companion to go for an ice cream cone in the middle of the day, count Gene out.

"Not really," I said lightly. "I just—I don't know, I thought I heard something the other night. When I was working late."

"Hmm," he said. "You sure it wasn't just T-om with a new mantra?"

I laughed. "Probably," I said. "I just wanted to mention it. In case . . . well, just in case."

"I will be especially vigilant," he said.

Then I took my plastic bagful of menace to the police station two blocks south.

The Grace station is basically one big room with desks for each officer, a communications bank of multicolored wires for the dispatcher, and a glassed-off corner for Chief Thaddeus Belgium. Both Easy's and Burrows's desks were vacant that morning, but the Chief's cubicle was overflowing. I spotted Jackson Kellermyer, the Island County Sheriff; Frank Lautenberg and Claude Forbush, Chiefs of the Port Angelina and Sweetbay police forces, respectively; and Captain Truman Newell from the Orson Naval Base. All of them seemed to be talking at once, and all looked grim.

I detoured to Ellie's desk instead. Ellie Foster is the dispatcher for all emergency services on East Island, as our half is known. Nine-one-one calls come in to this switchboard, and Ellie dispatches police, fire, ambulance, or whatever else is needed. Her counterpart on the West Island is Barbara Rose Bingham. Like secretaries in most any office you could name, they run the business while the Big Guns (such as those now wrangling in Chief Belgium's office) fight for their jurisdictions.

I am not comfortable with the standard P.I. practice of cultivating people in strategic positions for informational purposes, but Ellie is a genuine friend. We hit it off early in my residence on the island and have regular lunch dates. So I do call on her from time to time, though I make a point of reciprocating the service.

Ellie looked startled to see me. "You're not still in the hospital?"

I patted about my body. "Guess not."

"I thought you were in a coma."

"No more than usual."

"Yeah, joke, Molly," Ellie said angrily, "but I was worried sick about you. Easy said your identity was being kept a secret, but—"

I hugged her head. "I'm sorry, love, I guess I'm still whistling in the dark."

"They said you were in a coma and couldn't have visitors."

"I was only out a day, and it was never a coma; that was for the press. But if even you didn't know, I guess it's working. In fact, you don't see me at all. I just stopped in to give something to the Chief, then I'm off to Seattle on a case of my own. I am officially comatose until the creep is caught."

I set the plastic bag I'd transferred the thing into on her desk. "I found this yesterday at the cabin, near the pyre. Looks to me like he probably tried to use it before the nail, as in drive a stake into the witch's heart, but he couldn't get it sharp enough. He didn't do much better Saturday night in Emerald."

She stared at it, drawing back slightly from the bag. "Jesus," she said. "But why here?"

"Why not? Apparently the man has begun to travel. Seattle, then the island, Emerald . . . Next, who knows? Look how many states Bundy managed to terrorize."

Then Ellie's gaze focused behind me and I turned to see Chief Belgium approaching.

"You look pretty good for a comatose," he said, with about as close as he comes to a smile.

"Yeah. Thanks for keeping the media off my back. That's all I'd need; my client's already threatening to sue for desertion."

His gaze shifted to the bag on Ellie's desk.

"Something I found at the scene," I said, "on my run yesterday. In Emerald he used a knife but still didn't get them sharp enough."

He picked it up, rotating the bag to see the contents from all sides. Thad Belgium is a large man, thick, with near-white hair that doesn't match his bushy black beard. An exile from L.A. who managed to escape with his humanity, he's a big fish in a small pond. Most of the time he seems distracted, not quite present, but when he focuses, he can be brilliant.

"Might have been better to leave it where you found it," he said gruffly.

Or he can be an ass.

"The pyre had already collapsed. The wood was scattered pretty much at random."

Without looking at me he said, "You were at the Emerald scene, then, Saturday night?"

"Yeah. Found a couple there like this, sharpened with a knife, but apparently still not strong enough to penetrate. That's why I started looking. A nail just didn't make sense, not the way this guy thinks. A knife either."

"I'll have the county lab check it out." Then he looked at me, still frowning. "Tell me you didn't handle any of this."

"I didn't handle any of this."

He raised the bag again to eye level, staring at the flattened ends. "Thank God she was already dead," he said.

CHAPTER 16

NATURE'S MOTOR SEEMED to have accelerated, for the day was heating up fast. I caught the nine-thirty ferry on the brink of departure and headed for the bow, wanting the good salt air on my face to drive out the images of fire and pain. It felt good to be moving again. I was glad I had my own case to occupy my mind; otherwise, I probably would be obsessing about the Crucifixer. And his were images I wanted as far from my mind as I could push them. For me, the secret to not getting stuck is, simply, to keep moving.

Last on, I was last off in Port Condor and had to be content with following the parade through its strange mix of yachts and mobile homes until we hit the edge of town and began to go our separate ways. It was well past rush hour, so traffic on Highway #525 was relatively thin, as was Interstate 5 until the northern boundary of Seattle loomed, where drivers were enjoying one of my least favorite games: seeing how close they could get to the cars in front of them without slowing down. A sort of quasiadult form of chicken. Some of my most colorful language is expressed at such times.

The address on Harley's check had to be in the northwest quadrant of Seattle, so I began with that. I hadn't found a 19th Avenue N.W. on my map, but it couldn't be hard to find, I figured. It had to be between 15th and 20th Avenues, N.W., right?

Except that when I crossed the county line at North 205th Street, I went up one north–south street and down another from 8th Avenue to Richmond Beach and found no 19th Avenue N.W.

My vocabulary was reaching new lows by the time I gave up and sought the help of a Texaco station. Their employees, however, must be required to know only locales in Texas, for I got no further than "Must be around here somewhere." I decided to use their pay phone instead.

The phone number on the check at least rang—ergo, existed—but the elderly voice that answered after four rings assured me he was not nor ever had been Harley Abbott.

"May I ask how long you've had this number?" I said, trying to keep hope alive.

"Ever since we been here. Near thirty years now."

"Can you remember ever getting calls for a Harley Abbott before?"

"Well, not that I—"

I could hear another voice in the background, a tremulous woman's voice. Then the man came back on. "What was that name?"

I repeated it. There was more discussion between the two voices, then the female came on the line.

"Who is this?"

I paused, as I always do, to be sure honesty would be the best policy in the situation, decided yes, and told her my name and profession, rattling off the certification number for good measure. Older people, I'd noticed, tend to be impressed with anything that sounds even remotely like the law. Unlike my generation, who are more likely to proclaim their rights and hang up.

"Well, this is Anna Lutz," she said, firmly but respectfully. "And I do remember somebody calling once for that name. I remember because the woman was so nasty when I said I didn't know such a person."

I was about to ask if she could possibly remember when that was, when she went on without prompting.

"It must have been about twenty-four years ago, because that's when our first grandchild was born. Our Emmy's husband was over there in Vietnam, so she was here with us. He never did come back, God rest his soul, but she's remarried now and got three more, so—"

The man's voice said something querulous in the background, then Mrs. Lutz said indignantly, "Well, like I was saying, this woman did call for somebody—I think it was that name—and wasn't she fit to be tied when we said we didn't know any such gentleman. She carried on like you would not—"

"Did she give her name?"

"Well, I guess she did, if you could believe her. She said if I ever did speak to that man—mind you, she said some words about him that I would not repeat—she said I should tell him that his wife had called and next thing she was going to call her lawyer."

"But he's never been in touch with you?"

"No, he hasn't. This is the first time I heard that name since that day."

I thanked her very much, however scant the information was in balance. It was no great surprise, after all, that Shirleen Abbott had a bad mouth. Or that the marriage had been less than amicable. I was still left, like her, holding an empty dance card. I'd run down the social-security number on the check as a matter of course, but my hopes for it were nil.

Actually, I was surprised I'd never run into the dodge before. Had anybody ever asked for any identification when I'd opened a bank account? You filled out the form and they put it on the checks. The possibilities for chicanery were endless. It did, however, boost my respect for the man; apparently he was not just another pretty face.

All of which was getting me nowhere. As solace I treated myself to a full breakfast. Usually, I'm so antsy to get going in the morning that I'm doing well if I grab a bowl of granola and eat it on the run. That day I hadn't even stopped for o.j., my to-do list was so long. I'd spotted a Palace of Pancakes a few blocks from my dead end, so I headed back to it: time and fuel to regroup and figure out my next plan of attack.

Not one to do anything by halves, I ordered *The Works: 2 eggs any way you want them, 3 strips crispy bacon or savory sausage, 3 of our light and luscious pancakes. See flavors below.*

The *flavors below* included nut and honey, maple and pecan, chocolate chip and whipped cream, and the one I chose, strawberry and ricotta. I said no thank you to coffee; I was wired enough.

While I waited, I rethought my schedule. Visiting the address from the I.R.S. was the logical next step. I dug in my bag and set the two addresses side by side. One was in the Northwest sector, the other southeast; so why . . . ?

I slid out of the brown Leatherette booth and went in search of a phone book.

The two pay phones were in the short corridor that led to the rest rooms, but both chains hung bookless, so I approached the counter and squeezed between a hefty man and the adjoining stool to ask the waitress if I might borrow a phone book from their office.

She gestured with her head toward the other end of the counter, scooped up two dimes and the plate and cup beside them, and headed for the waitress station.

The woman displayed in the doorless office was alarmingly obese, her arms swelling out of the short sleeves of her unironed cotton blouse and lying in a roll beneath her armpits. I was beginning to regret the pancakes order.

"Pardon me?" I said when she did not look up. "I wonder if I could trouble you for a look at your phone book."

She stared at me with no change of expression. Then she said, "Damn people. They steal everything they can lay their hands on."

The statement didn't seem to be directed at me, so I waited silently for her reply.

She reached into the right side of her desk where a deep drawer once had been and brought up one book after another: a fat volume of white pages and two for yellow, one *A–L*, the other *M–Z*. "Don't know what you want," she said.

"I'd really appreciate all three. I'll be having a large breakfast [to assure her I was a patron] and I'd like to study them while I eat." Then, to her skeptical look, I added, "I won't steal them, I promise."

She shrugged and made a dismissive gesture with the hand that held the pen. I hefted the three books, which reached to my chin, and carried them back to my booth.

My breakfast had already arrived, and from across

the room the waitress gave me a peeved look meant to shame me for letting it get cold. Everybody's a mom.

My mouth full of egg, I started with the introductory listings in the white pages, going through city, county, and state listings for every possible locale, but found no zip-code map.

One turned up, finally, in the opening pages of the *A–L* volume and confirmed my suspicion that the two addresses couldn't possibly have the same zip code. And the one given on both was the correct number for the Southwest address, which made me suspect that at one time at least he had lived in that sector. I made an outline on my own map of the boundaries indicated for that zip code and spent the rest of the time it took to sin with strawberries and cheese copying down addresses and phone numbers for key agencies—Social-Security Office, Department of Motor Vehicles, Small Business Administration, and various other licensing agencies in city, county, and state. Then I dutifully returned the volumes and hit the streets.

When I approach an address I have any reason to believe might become a site for future surveillance, I take care not to leave my car within sight of the house, so it won't be recognized if I decide to stake out the place. My car, while not flashy, is not nondescript either. The '86 Honda Civic is the color of peanut butter on top, chocolate on the bottom, a custom job for the woman I bought it from when I arrived in Washington State. I suspected her of Reese's Cup addiction.

The last thing you want to be on a stakeout, of course, is conspicuous. I know I should have repainted the thing an invisible-by-night black by now. But I was taken by the color combo (no Reese's slouch myself) and haven't yet been able to talk myself into doing the reasonable thing. So on stakeouts I try to keep it out of sight by day and away from streetlights at night.

It was after noon when I approached the southside address Mrs. Thomas had given Mary Alice. The area had gone almost entirely industrial, only a few small houses left to suggest it had ever been anything else. My hopes were dwindling with each block. So it was a pleasant surprise to find an actual house with the actual number on the actual street for the address I had, and I cruised slowly past it, then turned right at the next cross street, then right again, and parked at a distance roughly parallel with the targeted house in the next block, then reversed my path on foot.

I barely glanced at the house, because to its right, down a wide gravel driveway, stood a steel-clad garage that looked big enough to house several trucks. Twice as wide as the small one-story house and nearly twice as high, the building might once have been an auto repair shop, but now it looked closed up tight—overhead door down, no visible windows. And if it was only a private garage, one thing it was not housing was the ratty little phlegm-green sedan that was pulled off onto the lawn on the far side of the drive.

As I approached on foot, the garage loomed to dominate the house, extending all the way to the property line, which was marked by a chain-link fence, beyond which stretched the asphalt parking lot of Sammy's Southside Machine Shop.

I paused to look at the house a moment before I went up the walk. Its front door was off-center, about two-thirds to my left, and there was a narrow window in that section, a bathroom perhaps. There was another window in the wider section, both hung with yellowing venetian blinds closed up tight.

Weeds almost covered the flagstone path that led

to steep concrete steps, up to an unroofed concrete stoop before the door—not the most inviting layout I'd ever seen. But I walked it and, seeing no bell, knocked on the dark-green door, at a spot even more worn of paint than the rest of the house's face, presumably by previous knockers.

No response. I listened for any sounds of movement from inside, but heard nothing. I repeated the knocks and waited, listening, twice more before I decided I'd been given permission to browse.

I headed straight for the garage along a well-worn tangent across the scruffy lawn. The door, I now saw, was not only shut down but padlocked to a ring sunk into concrete at its midsection. Either this was an area with serious burglary problems, I concluded, or somebody was paranoid about whatever lay inside.

There was no window on the side of the building facing the house, so I rounded the other side, but found it windowless as well. As I approached the rear, its shallow dirt yard also fenced with chain link, I was greeted with the sight of enough monstrous tires, rusted metal parts, and junk machinery to furnish an avant-garde sculpture garden. But there was a window—small, set high in the back wall of the building, but a window nonetheless.

I was just plotting my ascent when I heard a scraping sound from the house and looked to see a woman, her head and one shoulder poked out of the crack between sliding glass doors in the back of the house.

I turned and headed toward her, smiling as though this was the customary way to approach a house. I hadn't gone six feet, though, before the sliding door scraped shut again, and I heard the rasp of a metal bolt and the clunk of its lock.

I kept going, still smiling, and mounted the shallow concrete slab of patio before the door.

The woman inside, barely visible in the crack between heavy drapes, was frail, wrapped in a cheap cotton robe, her pale hair flat on one side as though she'd just left a bed. She held a wadded handkerchief that covered her nose and mouth beneath staring, frightened eyes.

"I'm sorry if I startled you," I called to her, loud enough, I hoped, to carry through the glass.

She gave no sign of having heard, or maybe understood, what I'd said, so I charaded sliding open the door again, still smiling my most harmless smile.

She shook her head. So I raised my voice even further. "I'm looking for Harley Abbott," I called. "Does he live here?"

I could tell by the widening of her dark eyes that she recognized the name, even as she began shaking her head vigorously.

"Did he used to live here? Do you know where he can be found?"

More head-shaking, and she made a motion with the hand not holding the hanky that my mother uses with the word *scoot*.

I tried another tack. "Is your husband at home?"

This time the negative shake was accompanied by a thin voice and the words, "No. You go. He come soon." I couldn't pinpoint the accent, but it sounded Eastern European.

I figured that was as far as I was going to get, so I backed away, still smiling, and started around the side of the house toward the front, giving a last longing look at that high garage window. I think the operant psychology is similar to the effect of a veil on a woman's face, exciting lust in the hearts (or wherever) of prurient men.

My preoccupation nearly made me bump into a mailbox mounted on a stake at the corner of the house. I looked up to see if I was being observed, and seeing no movement of the plain olive cotton cloth covering the only window on this side of the house, I stuck my hand in as fast as any at a cookie jar and withdrew the contents. I had the two envelopes nearly to my jacket pocket, in fact, before some of my upbringing caught up with me, and I only looked at the addressee before shoving them back in the box and continuing to undo my trespass.

Both envelopes—one a window, probably a bill, the other looking generated by a computer—were addressed to Carl Erchak.

CHAPTER 17

I BACKTRACKED ALONG THE SIDEWALK, wondering what, if anything, my new knowledge meant. The woman—Mrs. Erchak, presumably—had recognized the name Harley Abbott, and she was scared. But was that what she was afraid of? She'd locked herself in *before* I mentioned the name. With the security precautions on the garage, maybe it was only crime in the neighborhood she feared. I wished I knew Seattle better. In my ten months in the biz, I'd been to the city on a search only once, and it was brief, in a University-area middle-class neighborhood. I knew very little about the crime topography elsewhere.

But I couldn't help feeling that some important clue(s) to my search for Alice Abbott lay at an address where Harley Abbott *might* have lived two decades ago or more and was determined to get a look into that garage. I couldn't seem to shake the notion that those three trucks Shirleen Abbott had apparently bought for her husband *after* he left were a key to the dead end so far of Harley Abbott in the year 1979.

I got back in my car and headed for the nearest gas station with a pay phone. I'd intended to visit several agencies on an information search that afternoon. But

Mrs. Erchak had said her husband would be home "soon," and whenever there was a choice between first- and secondhand information, I went with the direct route every time. The bureaucracies would just have to deal with my voice alone today.

I found an Amoco station three blocks south and filled my tank before I used the phone. The day had begun to get unseasonably hot, and I watched the rainbow puddle of gas below the hose hookup shimmer with heat fumes.

I paid, got a pocketful of quarters, and pulled up next to the pay phone at the back of the lot. I pulled the pad from my bag and took a moment to lay out my strategy.

It has been my—albeit brief—experience that, of all the many guarded bureaucracies, the social-security offices have the toughest doors to get a foot into. Even if I had better visual credibility as a private investigator, it's unlikely I could get the information I needed with an upfront approach. So I've developed a few characters to do the work for me more . . . indirectly. It is one of the advantages to being a private as opposed to a police detective. If you're a cop, dissembling is discouraged, unless you're part of a decoy or sting operation that has upper-echelon approval. But us freelancers can get away with a reasonable amount of deception in a righteous cause.

That day I decided to be Wendy calling the social-security office to check out Harley's number. I assigned no credibility whatsoever to the number on the check, but they were as good as any other nine digits from which to start. The social-security number is the sine qua non for entrée into almost any other file, its possession the proof of your legitimacy.

Wendy Duling is a character to be used with caution, and I've even changed identities on the spot if the voice on the other end of the line sounded like someone who would be irritated by her into silence. She is one of that alarming number of women not much younger than myself who seem compelled to end every sentence on a quizzical upswing. After all the assertiveness training absorbed by the generation ahead of us, the trend feels like a regression toward perpetual tentativeness. But however lacking Wendy may be in authoritative force, she makes up for in nonthreatening deference. It's hard to feel pushed by someone who questions every word out of her mouth. So she often can get information that's withheld from someone who sounds more aggressive.

The answering voice at Seattle's downtown social-security office, which identified itself as Carol, sounded as kindly as a seasoned bureaucrat is likely to get, so I tried Wendy.

"Hi, this is Wendy, Wendy Duling, from the city clerk's office? How are you doing today?"

She was doing all right.

"We have this little puzzle here I hoped you'd be able to help us out with? This woman, Mary Alice Abbott? Her father, Harley Abbott, was killed in an awful car crash last month, and she's come in about the death certificate, for the insurance? But the social-security number she has for him is one we already have on file for somebody else, so I don't know which one's the right one, you know?"

She asked for the one I had, and I gave her the number printed on the check.

She wasn't gone long before she came back to ask for Harley's birth date. Oops. From the age on the marriage certificate I had the year, but no month or day.

"Gee, I didn't ask for the exact date, and she's down having coffee right now? But she did say he was fifty. Is that enough for you to find him?"

"Hmm. I think maybe I know where your mistake lies. We do have a Harley Abbott close to that number, but one digit off." She read the number. "But according to our records, he's forty-seven, not fifty."

"Wow, I'm sure you're right. Thanks, Carol, thanks a lot."

I hung up, feeling both proud of my ploy and amazed at the outcome. The guy had changed only one digit. Cocky bastard. That could make him easier to track, pride goething before a fall as it tends to. And forty-seven would have made him only twenty in the wedding photo. Guess they both fudged, in opposite directions. Pride and vanity both.

With social-security number in hand, along with the registration certificates for Harley's three trucks, I called the Seattle DMV, guessing on the south-side office. Presumably, I'd have a right to the information I was seeking. But the DMV comes in a close second to social security in defending their turf and are not fans of the Right to Information Act. So I decided to play it safe and call as Agnes Parr, the equally wary, acronym-weary veteran of the auditor's office.

I'd raised my voice a couple of notes for Wendy; now I lowered it for Agnes and dropped the lilt.

"Afternoon," I said to the voice that had answered only, "DMV."

"This is Agnes, tax auditor's office. We're going over some questionable records here from Island County, and we've got these 420-002's that are dead-ended, far as I can tell. Titles on three trucks listing Shirleen Abbott as legal owner, town of Grace, Prince Island, Harley Abbott registered owner, Southwest Seattle. But we don't have taxes paid on those vehicles for almost twenty years and the address is bogus. Could you see what current address you've got for him? Looks like we'd better round him up and get some money out of him."

The terse DMV voice asked for the number of Harley's driver's license. I had to bite my tongue to keep from saying that, if I had that, I probably wouldn't have needed to call. Instead, I told him that the certificate of title didn't give it, but I had his social-security number, which I recited.

There was a considerable wait before the voice came back on the line to say that they had no current information whatsoever on a Harley Abbott. The driver's license they had for him—a commercial license, same social-security number—had been due for renewal in 1980 but had never been renewed.

Through my disappointment I thought to ask for their last address but was not surprised to hear the one I'd just left.

Eager to get back there, since it seemed to be the end of the trail, I made only one more call, to the Teamsters Local #741. I phoned as myself, thinking I hadn't much to lose, and told them what I knew and didn't know. But their information went no further than the DMV's. He'd been a line driver with the union beginning in 1975 but had become "inactive" in 1979, and they had no record of him since.

Feeling somewhat defeated, I got back in my car and took off for the Erchaks' again. I was determined to see the insides of that garage before I declared the trail totally cold.

CHAPTER 18

I WAS NEARLY TO THE HOUSE, planning to cruise past as I had before, when I spied through the heavy boughs of a drooping spruce two figures who looked as though they were coming down those steps. I jammed on the brakes and pulled to the side.

They hadn't noticed me. The giant of a man—he looked seven feet, easy—was pulling the slight woman by the arm, his face grim, while she wailed something in a Slavic-sounding language. She was still wearing the housecoat and slippers I'd seen her in, fast-shuffling to keep up with his long strides.

For a minute I hoped he might be about to raise the garage door, but he strode on past it to the old green sedan and half-flung her toward the passenger's side while he folded himself into the driver's seat.

He'd started the car by the time she got in, and the door slammed shut as he backed the car in a sharp counterclockwise arc, then gunned it onto the gravel of the drive and out into the street, taking off in the opposite direction from where I sat.

I debated for a moment whether to follow them or put their absence to good purpose. Since the green car had been already there when I was, Erchak—whom I assumed the big man to be—must have arrived in something else which, since not visible, must be in that garage.

They were gone too fast to give me time to change my mind, but I knew I'd have opted for snooping anyway. Let's face it: P.I.'s may have a streak of taxi driver in them (as in, "Follow that car!"), but mostly we're just plain snoopy, peeking into private places, both figuratively and literally, sniffing out the secrets. So I backed my car up until I was sure it could not be seen from the premises, then got out and locked it. Then unlocked it, in case I needed to make a quick getaway.

The window in the back wall of the garage looked higher and smaller than I remembered it. But as such, I figured it would not be locked. Why, a person would have to be as small as, say, four-foot-nine and reasonably slim to stand a chance of squeezing through that opening. I was just hoping those dimensions would do it. If not, I could still peek.

The tires in the scattering of junk I'd seen in the back were enormous, reaching nearly to my chin as I wrestled one up on edge and rolled it to the wall, then let it flop down again. Naturally, it didn't flop just where I wanted and had to be maneuvered up and down and over until it lay at the optimum position beneath the window. It was followed by another, the task of pivoting the thing into place nothing compared to supporting its weight at an angle to work it up and over the first one. My right shoulder—the one that had taken the bullet in Chicago—was soon letting me know loud and clear that it did not approve of this activity.

Three proved to be the stacking limit, and I had to find other debris to add to the pile until it was high enough for me to clamber up and come within eyeshot of the lower edge of the window frame.

By then it was 3:37 by my watch, and the afternoon sun hit the filthy glass of the window at such an angle that most of what I could see inside was a hazy glare. All I could make out were three large shapes standing side by side between walls loaded with automechanic paraphernalia.

The window was ajar and opened inward, like a hatch. I studied it and decided I could probably squeeze through, despite the pancakes of the morning.

I descended twice more and dragged and propped and pushed two more choice pieces of debris onto the pile before I could make it elbow-high to the edge of the window.

There were not three trucks inside. But there was the cab of one that looked big enough to pull a train. I'd always felt bullied by trucks, in my hatchback far below. But the head of this thing was no farther than six feet from my face, and I recoiled instinctively. Its snout was short, beneath smoked-glass windows, and cut with a shiny vertical grill I tried not to think of as a sinister grin.

Get a grip, I told myself. It's not the inanimate objects that are the problem.

There was barely room in the huge garage for the three of them: the cab on my right, a windowless box trailer in the middle that stood even taller than the cab, and a long flatbed on the left, its wheels on the twin tracks of a hydraulic lift that still sat at ground level. The three of them hooked together would have measured at least forty feet.

The box was an easy jump beneath me if I could just make it through the window. I tried shoving the window farther up and inward and nearly succeeded in pushing myself off the torn navy vinyl car seat that was my perch at the top of the pile. Wiping sweat from my grimy face, I reminded myself to move slowly and carefully if I wasn't to topple the whole stack and me with it onto the ground, which now looked very far below me.

I braced my forearms on the sharp lower edge of the aluminum window frame and hoisted my body until I was balanced at the waist halfway in. I had a passing fantasy of launching myself into a swan dive that would climax in a perfect four-point landing on the trailer, but the actual execution proved a good deal less graceful. Mostly I just wiggled and wrenched and battered my way under the angled window until I was more in than out, then thrust my body forward with my hands and landed with a smack on the hood of the huge box.

Once my breath came back to me, I peered around the shadowy spaces of the garage, lit only by the daylight coming through that one high window. Still, I could see that unlike the clutter outside, the shabby green car, and the forlorn-looking house, the interior of the garage seemed in perfect order. Pegboard covered the right-hand wall, hung with polished tools, while shallow shelves along the left wall held row after row of white boxes that presumably held the smaller nuts and bolts of equipment maintenance. Standing below, like polite visitors, I identified several pneumatic jacks, air pumps, and a row of guns I hoped held only oil.

But it was the cab I was determined to get into, to see what telltale paperwork it might contain. Looking down at the door, I was glad I was starting the task from above rather than below. I couldn't even have reached the handle from the floor; whereas when I knelt on the box and peered down at the smoked glass, I could see that the window on my side was rolled nearly three-quarters of the way down, enough for me to slither through easily.

It didn't prove quite that easy, to tell the truth, but I'll spare the embarrassing details. Suffice it to say that I got in with only a small rip to the seat of my jeans.

I went straight for the glove compartment and pulled out in turn a hefty flashlight, windshield cleaner and (clean) chamois cloths, and enough packets of vehicle information to stock a workshop.

It was only after that bulk had been cleared away that I found the kind of informational treasure I was looking for: Two business-size envelopes were labeled with bold block letters, one reading OWNERSHIP, the other EXPENSES.

If I'd have used my head at that point, I'd have tucked the envelopes into the waistband of my jeans and gotten out of there the same way I came in. Larceny is not to be taken lightly, but the consequences of discovery can be a lot heavier.

Naturally, I didn't do the sensible thing. I *had* to see into that ownership envelope—then, not later. So I dug into it right there.

There were several documents in the envelope, two of them the same sort of five-by-eight certificates of registration I'd found tucked under Shirleen's box spring. I had to use the flashlight to decipher them in the dim light of the garage.

The earliest-dated document was a duplicate of the one listing Shirleen as Legal Owner and Harley as Registered Owner. On the second, dated two years later, Harley's name did not appear. Instead, the legal—and registered—owner was listed as one Roman Marcello, and there was a bill of sale attached, passing ownership from her to him for the cab, box, and trailer, at this address.

So Harley was now out of the picture? I wondered, with a pang of disappointment. Then I remembered that this used to be Harley's address, and from the reaction of the woman who now lived here, the connection had not been entirely severed. Unless the jolly giant had murdered Harley and copped his property.

But who was this Roman Marcello, and how did he figure into the equation?

The name came up again in the fourth document from the envelope, a lease agreement between Roman Marcello, listed as Owner of the three-part rig, and Carl Erchak, listed as Lessee. It was dated a little over a year ago, and gave a different address in Seattle, different zip code, for Marcello.

It was at that point that I heard a mufflerless motor and the crunch of gravel, indicating that Mr. and Mrs. Carl Erchak had returned.

"Shit!" I said aloud. Why hadn't I just taken the damn things and read them later?

In some sort of gesture of atonement, I shoved the documents back in the OWNERSHIP envelope and put both envelopes and the rest of the contents back in the glove compartment, taking time only to commit to memory the address given for Roman Marcello. Then I snapped the compartment shut and concentrated on willing the footsteps I now heard on the drive to continue past the garage into the house.

Which they did, thank the patron saint of burglars. But I still wasted no time in scooting out of the cab, opening the door and turning on my belly to slide down off the seat until I was dangling by my grip on the door frame, then letting myself drop to the concrete below.

I know how to fall as well as the next guy, bending the knees and all that. But a six-foot drop to an ungiving surface is a substantial jolt, and my spine was still reverberating when I heard heavy steps approaching from the direction of the house.

I said several more choice words and looked around frantically for a hiding place. This did not seem an appropriate time and place for an introduction to this player in my puzzle: "Hi, I just dropped in (your window) for a chat." I now wished I'd thought as much about my way out through that window as in.

I heard the jerk of the padlock on its metal ring, then a series of clicks, indicating a combination being run that left me only seconds. There was nothing for it, I guessed, but to go horizontal again. The box beside me was mounted on three sets of double wheels, about five feet apart, lifting the bed maybe a foot and a half off the floor. I dropped to the concrete and slid under, just as the door was being raised with a great screeching of joints.

My anxiety level here was a good deal greater than it had been under Shirleen's bed. For one thing, there was that peach dust ruffle to conceal me. For another, however poisonous the lady's tongue might be, she didn't present much of a physical threat: I could have taken two of her at once. But this guy—whose size-twenty-or-so sand-color desert boots now pounded along not two feet from my face—was quite another matter. His body language as he hustled along his frail wife had left me with the distinct impression that this was not a man whose wrath it would be wise to incur.

He clumped down to the other end of the box under which I was hiding and did some clanging of metal. I craned my neck around to follow his boots and was glad to see that whatever he was doing, he was not doing it at my level.

He was soon finished, and walked around the front of the cab to the driver's side and hoisted himself in, with a good deal less effort than it had taken me. This, I thought, was a good sign: He apparently intended to drive the thing off, leaving me to exit the way I'd entered.

But that would have been too easy, wouldn't it, leaving me with no lesson learned to change my burgling ways. Instead, he backed the cab out of the garage to the street—at an astonishing speed—then turned it around and backed it straight at my hiding place.

My stomach did several sickening churns as the tow equipment on the back of the cab came rushing into view, looking way too phallic for my psychic comfort. By now I was sweating heavily and felt lightheaded from the airless heat of the garage and from a chemical odor I'd been smelling ever since I dropped into the place, but which now was stronger, seeming to ooze from the box above. The puke odor of sulfur was the only ingredient I recognized, but I'd smelled the same thick scent from several factory smokestacks in the area.

Erchak dropped from the cab and lumbered over to the coupling device, confirming my fear that he meant to hook up the box and drive it right off me, leaving me exposed in this ridiculous position.

I raised my head slightly and did a quick check of the underbelly of the box above me, fore and aft. Between my feet and the front of the box was a shelf on which two spare tires lay side by side. Just behind my head was a large metal cylinder—spare gas tank, I guessed. Maybe for its protection, two heavy bars extended from one end of the box to the other, passing under the tank and extending under the shelf.

If only they were closer together, I thought, I could hook my arms and legs around them and hitch my body up clear of the ground, at least until I was out of the garage. Then I could drop off and just hope he wasn't looking in his rearview mirror at the time, at least long enough for me to roll out of his view.

Trouble was (among other things), the bloody bars were way wider apart than my elbows could reach—almost beyond the reach of my hands.

The truck's motor was deafening; it was hard for me to think while the sound was bombarding my head in the echoing garage. Maybe I should just stay where I was, I thought, and let the box be driven off me, then quickly conceal myself.

I looked at the flatbed on my left, but the tracks of the lift blocked any possibility of rolling under that. And to my right the empty space left by the cab's removal was totally exposed.

Besides, I felt more dread, when it came down to it, of being locked in the garage without the box to help me reach the window than I did of taking my chances on an open playing field. I had visions of stacking up everything in the place to reach the window, then having the pile outside topple, leaving me no way to get down. And even if I got out, there would be the pile here to let Erchak know someone had been inside. Since I'd put the contents of the glove compartment back when I heard him drive up, there was nothing to indicate that his security had been breached if I rode this thing out, then went back to dismantle the other pile before I made my getaway.

The question was quickly becoming moot, as Erchak seemed to have finished his hookup operation and was heading back to the cab. I wriggled haunch after haunch, moving my body down toward the front of the box, and tried to find a toehold for my feet on the shelf with the spare tires. My legs wouldn't reach to the outside of the tires, but I found a lip above the shelf I could hook my toes on, and spread my legs until my heels were wedged between the lip and the tires. Then I stretched my arms as far as they would go to see what grip I could get on those bars.

Spread-eagled like that, I felt about as vulnerable as any female could feel, but by the time the box began to move, I at least moved with it.

As we cleared the walls of the garage, I turned my head back and forth on a neck already beginning to ache from the strain. To my left, the spruce behind which I'd concealed the car looked very far away, and to my right, there was nothing between the drive and the house, which looked even more like a shut-tight box than it had that morning. I felt a surge of empathy with the woman in that house, as trapped, it seemed, as I felt now.

The cab was almost to the street by the time the end of the box cleared the garage and Erchak got down to go lock it again. As the sound of his footsteps approached, I had another flash of panic. Was there any way he could see me from the back of the box when he turned after lowering the garage door? My head wouldn't turn that far.

But the footsteps returned after the lowering of the door, and I tried to turn my mind to more useful topics, like how to get myself out of this mess. I closed my eyes, trying to picture a scenario in which I could drop off the box and escape without being run over by the wheels behind me or detected in the huge rearview mirrors that flanked the cab's snout. It seemed a little late for a pact with God never to be so reckless again, but I put it out anyway.

The turning maneuverability of the long box was considerably more limited than that of the cab; that became evident with the truck's first right-hand turn onto the street. By the time the back wheels were engaged, the box was moving on a diagonal tangent across the corner of the yard, and I saw the curb only moments before the wheels bumped down it, nearly knocking me off my precarious perch.

I allowed myself an "Aaargh!" as the box landed, knowing the noise of the motor would drown out anything I could produce, including cries for help.

Again I had to lecture myself to reason: This guy might not be thrilled about my breaking into his garage if he found out, but it wasn't a crime punishable by death. *Overdramatizing again, M.P. You just don't want to get caught with your hand in . . . whatever equivalent this is of the cookie jar.*

By now my right shoulder was threatening to detach, and every muscle in my body was screaming, *Just let go!* I dearly wished for my twelve-year-old body back, which could hang from anything, for any length of time, and still land on its feet, with a triple twist in between. I'd never realized just how old twenty-six is in the life of the body.

The rig was slowing for a stop sign, the first in the three blocks we'd traveled. *It's gotta be now,* I told myself, *this is as far as this bod can stick it.*

I looked left. There was no traffic passing on the two-lane street, but that could change at any moment and I wouldn't be able to see it coming until I was clear of the cab. It had to be to the right.

The asphalt expanse of a car wash was sliding by, a series of sheds with jets of soap and water bombarding the vehicles at their core, each sending gray rivulets down the slope of the wide drive to the street. No cover. But it was now or never.

As the cab braked to a halt, the trailing box bumped against its coupling, and my limbs released of their own accord. Eyes closed, I rolled to my right, between the wheels and across the lane, until I hit the curb and lay there, eyes still shut tight in that childhood conviction that if you can't see them, they can't see you.

Then the motor revved again and the rig lumbered away, leaving me huddled in the gutter, awash with soapy water that couldn't begin to clean off the grime.

My next concern was who might have seen me, and I lifted my head warily, gathering my limbs to stand. But the only people in sight were busy scrubbing their cars with brushes or rubbing them with soft chamois in the shelters of their domed sheds, and I picked myself up painfully and headed back in the direction from which I'd come.

I didn't even bother to hide my passing from the house in case the woman might be watching. I did circle the garage though, on the far side, and dismantled my makeshift stairway, nearly getting crowned as the navy car seat came tumbling down. I made no effort to put each piece back exactly as I'd found it—if I could have remembered where that was. The mess seemed to be in the past tense for Erchak, and I doubted he monitored its design.

Then I trudged back to my car, feeling more foolish than anything else. Bruised and strained and wet and grimy—and for what? I could hardly remember why I'd had any interest in those three stupid trucks in the first place.

I looked at my watch: 5:10. In little more than an hour I would be at Simon's, eating lobster. If I could just get past the butler looking like this.

CHAPTER 19

Harry Pound, along with his wife, Ursula, are kind of all-around caretakers of Simon's house and grounds. But Simon can't resist calling Harry "the butler." He's a short, square-cut man in his forties, with mild blue eyes and a sulky mouth that might have less to do with genetics than with the take-charge manner of his wife, whose Germanic accent can be heard clearly throughout the house with all doors shut.

Simon answers his own door, which is probably just as well, since Ursula would most likely have shut it in my face when she saw how disreputable I looked. But the pleased expression on Simon's face did not fade when he saw me, and he risked ruining his Harris tweeds by giving me the much-needed bear hug I always get from him.

In his early sixties, Simon Emmershaw looks typecast for the role of gentleman sleuth. A large man, now somewhat ruddy of face and swollen of paunch with good food and drink, his features are still strong, from a prominent chin to a broad brow, beneath a shock of pure white hair. Even the deep lines in his face seem more a product of character than age, and the keen blue eyes appear capable of seeing into your deepest secrets, though you're sure he'd be too well-bred ever to spill what he saw.

He drew me into the entrance hall and closed the door before he stood back to have a better look. "You didn't really have to dress for dinner," he said, deadpan. "Casual would have been sufficient."

I managed a small smile, while he stuck his head in the swinging door to the kitchen behind him and asked Ursula to run me a bath and find something clean for me to wear while my clothes were being washed.

Ursula replied tartly, at a volume that could have reached passersby on the street, "Not if you want soup. Cheese soup got to be stirred; can't stop or you get burned soup, got to throw it out. See where Harry is. Har-ree!"

I've never understood how or why Simon tolerates Ursula. He's a product of Vermont prep schools and summers in Europe, however he has deviated from that charted course since. His home, like his dress, says old money, and there's the kind of hush about it you find in museums. Into that hush, Ursula's raw voice slices like an electric knife through Camembert. Unless that's part of Simon's intent: to keep himself from too somnolent an existence. Simon and I don't speak of our private lives much, and never of our love lives, but I guess I'd be surprised to learn he had one, with either sex. There is something so balanced about him, so peaceful, and they don't call it sexual tension for nothing.

The echoes of Ursula's trumpeting had scarcely settled when Harry dutifully appeared through the back door to the garden and accepted Simon's mission. Meanwhile, I followed my host into the living room and perched on the edge of an unupholstered maple rocker—the only seat in the room that wouldn't be permanently fouled by my grubby bottom.

"So tell me what you're up to," Simon said from the brown leather lounger across from me. Simon hasn't exactly retired from the business, but I get the impression that his brain is the part of his body he uses most on any current case. He seems to enjoy hearing of my more physically adventuresome pursuits.

"I keep messing up," I said sourly.

He smiled, perhaps at the literal truth of the statement.

"I'm on this perfectly straightforward missing-persons case," I went on. "Nearly located her the first day out. But ever since I've gone haywire. Got myself clubbed at a murder scene; got so obsessed with trucks, I just literally let one roll over me—"

But Simon's mind had stopped at the first item on the list. "What murder scene? The Crucifixer? You're the one who's supposed to be comatose?"

" 'Fraid so," I said glumly. "I noticed the smoke in the woods when I got home that night and went rushing off to do my civic duty. Turned out to be a slightly more complex fire than I'd expected."

In my fatigue, Simon's concerned gaze was beginning to get to me; I could feel my eyes moistening. So I was relieved that Harry arrived at that moment to announce that my bath was ready.

Nearly an hour later I was seated by candlelight at Simon's twelve-foot walnut burl table in a clean white terry-cloth shaving robe, scarfing up lobster, Caesar salad, and Ursula's perfect unburned cheese and broccoli soup, sopped up with chunks of warm baguette. I could get used to this life, I thought. No wonder Simon bulges in the middle.

Between bites I filled him in on what little I knew

about the Crucifixer killings and my own tangential involvement with them on the island and in Emerald. Simon had been raised Catholic and was intrigued by the imagery, especially the stake-in-the-heart M.O. in the last two killings—details not released to the media.

What I really needed, though, was his clear thinking on my own case and over the Black Forest cake, I laid it out for him.

Simon is one of that fast-vanishing number of people who really listen. I think that's the key to why I never feel defensive around him, as I often do with other men who seem more interested in their own agendas than in anything I have to say. Feeling heard, I am ready to listen.

"What are your assumptions?"

It's a question he always asks, the first time adding, "If you have any, that's too many."

I always find I have too many.

"Well, I guess I believe my client is who she says she is."

"And who is that?"

"Both public and private identities, I guess. I sense there's a lot I don't know about her, but I suspect she doesn't either."

"The mother?"

"A real piece of work. Narcissism writ large. Treats the daughter like a servant, subtle put-downs. And not-so-subtle. The woman is the center of her own universe and seems to believe everyone else's should revolve around her. Mary Alice says she got religion in the past year, toned down, so I'd hate to have seen her before."

"And the uncle?"

"The bright star in Mary Alice's sky. He's a minor celebrity in Emerald, the weatherman for KEM news.

Hail-fellow-well-met. He's about three years younger than his sister, turns out, though he seems older. Very protective of them both.

"Another factor is the death of the parents: Mary Alice says her mother was thirteen when they died, some sort of accident. That would have made Wendell around ten. Must have had a big effect on them both."

"The protecting must have fallen to her in those years," Simon said.

I thought about it. "I guess. It's hard to see her in the role though. She certainly seems to have been a bust as a parent. Although in our initial interview Mary Alice said both her mother and her uncle protected her. Alice too."

"They protected Alice?"

"No, Alice protected her younger sister. That's what Mary Alice remembers about her, once she found out Alice was real and not just her imaginary friend as her mother'd been telling her all those years."

Simon looked as confused as I had been with the name-merger thing, and I repeated Mary Alice's theory that both names had been given to the second daughter when the first was evicted. "She apparently retained some memories though, and now they're starting to make sense to her."

Simon nodded gravely, his fingers propped together over his empty plate like a steeple, his jutting chin resting on the tips.

"So my focus now is on locating the ex-husband, Harley Abbott, Mary Alice's father. That's who Alice accuses in the letter of sexual abuse."

"And your client?"

"Abused? She has no such memories."

"That she knows of."

"That she knows of."

I went on to explain about the pictures I'd found and the packet with the marriage license application, the paperwork on the trucks, and the birth certificates.

"So the husband isn't the father of both girls."

"No, he couldn't be of Alice; he's too young. Shirleen could be preggy in the wedding picture, but that would be Mary Alice." I licked the last crumbs of cake from my fork.

"No lead on anyone else as the biological father?"

"No. The birth certificate just says *Unknown*."

"How about the uncle?"

"As the biological father? Well, I guess that happens, but he'd have to have been an awfully early bloomer. He couldn't have been more than eleven when Alice was born, judging from their childhood pictures."

"Of course. So you said."

"Apparently, Alice was pulled out of school in seventh grade. Her mother told the school she was being sent to live with her father. But, if so, she came back again, if she was there when Mary Alice was little. And she says in the letters that she was sent to some Bible-pounding woman. But she must have been around if she suspects Mary Alice's father of molesting her."

"You believe, then, that the husband is key to finding the older daughter."

"I can't think where else she'd go. Her last letter to Mary Alice sounded urgent, then she just disappeared. He's the one she accuses, and she came back, she says, to find out if he did the same to her little sister. When her meeting with Mary Alice didn't happen and she got fired from The Queen's Rest, maybe she thought it was confrontation time and took off to find him. Here, I'll get you the letters, see what you think."

I went to retrieve my bag in the hall, where it had

been hung on the brass umbrella stand, carefully away from all other soilable objects. The bag was faded denim, which I generally wore with the strap crossed left to right across my torso like a shoulder holster, hanging under my right arm to leave my hands free. When I'd affixed myself to the underbelly of the trailer, I'd centered it on my chest as buffer, and it was now streaked with grease that would never come out. One more casualty of the day.

I pulled open the drawstring neck, prepared for the worst, but was relieved to find the contents relatively intact and drew out the heavy manila envelope in which I'd stored the letters and other documents.

I took it back to Simon, still at the table. "They're all there," I said. "I'm going to call my office, see if there are any messages on the machine."

I used to try to pay Simon for any calls I made from his place to locales outside Olympia. But he wouldn't hear of it, so eventually I stopped. It wasn't, after all, as though it would strain his budget. Still, I felt uneasy with even that much of an exception to my pay-my-own-way lifestyle. That was what was on my mind as I heard my own voice at the other end of the line, hit the pounds symbol to bypass the message, then 575 to access any left for me.

There was only one: "This is Chief Belgium, Molly. Thought you might want to know that we've ID'd that victim out in your backyard. We got lucky on the prints: Juvy had her on record from the seventies. Name's Alice Abbott."

CHAPTER 20

IT WAS AT THAT MOMENT that I understood why people are told to sit down when they're about to receive shocking news. If there hadn't been Simon's footstool to drop onto, I'd have sunk to the floor. The blood drained from, then flooded my head with heat, and my mind began racing from one thought to another like a suddenly caged wild animal wondering what had just been done to its reality.

I placed the call again, although I could have repeated every word from memory. Alice? In my "backyard"? It could not have been a coincidence. Even within the relatively small space of Prince Island, to have murdered the object of my search, at the shack, the one I run past every morning—that could not have been a coincidence.

My hand moved of itself to the back of my head. Then my arrival at the scene could also have been anticipated, and he was waiting. In some unfathomable way we must both have been targeted by the Crucifixer. But how could that be? Did he stalk his victims well in advance? And still, how could he have known of the connection? Mary Alice had come to me only the day before, and Alice and I had never even met.

I don't know how long it was before I noticed Simon's legs standing beside the stool. I looked up.

"What is it?"

I told him.

He sat down, took my hand. We were both silent for a while, then Simon said, "What do you make of it?"

"I was about to ask you the same thing."

"Can you think of any ways your path might have crossed this man's before?"

"Before this case? I don't know what it could be. Unless it's my connection to Gray. But Alice. Why Alice? That has to be the link. And he didn't come after me directly; it was her he killed. How would he even know I'd see the smoke?"

The Ping-Pong ball of my brain was popping off in all directions. Could Alice have tailed Mary Alice to my office that first visit, then followed me home later? But what connection could that have with the killer? A massive headache was forming behind my eyes. I put my hand to my forehead.

"I think our first move should be to get you some sleep," Simon said.

"Fat chance," I said glumly.

"I've got some knockout drops that should do the trick," Simon said. "Tomorrow's plenty of time for your mind to be clear."

I looked at him. "You're a closet druggie? You never know, do you?"

"Doctor-prescribed," he said. "When the migraine medicine doesn't work. Come on, you need a good night's sleep. We can talk in the morning."

* * *

I have to admit, the little white pill did its thing—as far as it went. I was way under for the next ten hours, woke about six-thirty in the A.M. feeling woozy. The only trouble with drinking/drugging your troubles away is that eventually you have to wake up.

The first thought that made it through the Styrofoam of my head was not a thought but an image: of a body on a pyre surrounded by flames. Only this time the killer was there. I couldn't see who it was, but the figure was huge and held something aloft, the way victors brandish their weapons to announce their dominance.

It pissed me off, and I sat up, my jaw clenched half in fear, half in anger. The demon had thrown down the glove, and I was not going to back off.

My next thought was of Mary Alice. I'd all but forgotten her in last night's state of shock. What loss she must be feeling, to have almost had a sister, an ally, then to lose her before they'd even connected. I should have moved *faster*, I thought, then remembered that Alice must have been captured, if not already dead, before I'd even begun the search.

I'd have to call. Surely the police would have notified the family as soon as they'd identified the corpse. Alice's address would have been in the juvenile-court records. And if nothing else, Shirleen would have had to come clean finally about Alice's existence. It would be interesting to hear how she'd framed the story for Mary Alice; her version would doubtlessly be a whole lot different from Alice's. There was no question that I'd pursue the case with or without a client, but I at least should see what Mary Alice's wishes were at this point.

I gathered my limbs to get up, but they protested, claiming undue punishment the day before. So I moved rather more slowly, considerately, as I left the bed and put on the clothes that had been washed (so far as was possible) and laid on the antique chest of drawers while I was sleeping. Even the rip in the jeans had been mended. And I felt no loss that the University of Chicago sweatshirt would have to be discarded as soon as was modestly possible.

I descended toward the smell of batter and sausage and located a phone in the entry hall. I called Mary Alice's work number first. I knew how unlikely it was that she would be there, but I dreaded the prospect of getting her mother instead.

She wasn't. And I did.

Shirleen's voice was all teary, making three syllables of the word "He-el-lo?"

"Is Mary Alice there, please?" I tried to gravel my voice so she wouldn't recognize it.

"She is indisposed," Shirleen said, her voice stronger. "Who is this?"

My mind raced. Clearly, I should have prepared for this question. If I lied and were found out, it would be more suspicious than if I came out with it up front.

"It's Molly Piper, Mrs. Ab—Ms. Holman."

"Mary Alice is resting." She began tearing again. "We've had a death in the family."

"M-mm," I said. Now what did I do? I couldn't leave a number where Mary Alice could reach me, and I ought to talk to her, I thought, before I went much further with the case. "Actually," I said, "that's why I'm calling. I heard about your loss and wanted to see if there was anything I could do for Mary Alice. She's done so much for me."

I held my breath. Would I have known that Alice was the victim through any of the ordinary channels?

"How did you hear that it was our Alice?"

Shirleen said, harsh suspicion replacing the plaintive tone. "They haven't released the identity yet."

Merde. "My fiancé is Chief of Police in Emerald," I said, as smoothly as possible. I'd never had occasion to use the word *fiancé* before, but I hoped the overtones of respectability would help ease her suspicions. "He told me the last name was Abbott, because they had a Prince Island address for the victim and he thought I might know the family. So of course I thought of you, your family, and wanted to convey my condolences. If she was, in fact, a relative."

I knew I was babbling and was relieved to hear Mary Alice's voice in the background asking if the call was for her. She'd probably been waiting to hear from me, I thought.

Then Mary Alice came on the line. "Molly?" she said. "Have you heard?"

I told her how the news had come to me. "It must be such a shock," I said. "How are you doing?"

"Not too well, I'm afraid." Her tone was guarded.

"Can you talk? I could give you a number where you could reach me for the next hour or so, if you could get to a phone somewhere we could talk in privacy."

"I don't know . . ." she said doubtfully.

"Then maybe you could just tell me for now whether you want me to continue on the case, for whatever answers we might find."

"Yes," she said quickly. "Definitely, yes."

The firmness of her tone was new, making me wonder if she'd ever responded to anything with the word *definitely* before.

"I will then," I said, "and get in touch with you later. You could leave a message on my answering machine to tell me where and when would be a good time to talk. I have some things to report and hope to have more soon."

"Good," she said. "I have to know." Then, in a tone that broke my heart, "She was my Alice."

"Oh, Mary Alice," I said, "I'm so sorry. Sorry we didn't reach her first."

"Thank you," she said, her voice heavy with emotion. "Me too."

There remained a sort of echo in my head after I hung up the phone. *My Alice. Mary Alice.* Could the small child she was when her sister had been sent away have been told that she was calling her own name? Was she herself, in effect, her "imaginary friend"? At least she now had the confirmed knowledge of her sister's love to bolster that identity.

When I joined Simon in the dining room, he had already started on the walnut waffles and sausage I'd smelled from above. He called to Ursula for another batch, then looked at me quizzically to be sure the order was desired.

"Great," I said. "Thank you."

While I waited I ate grapes, one at a time, from my bowl of fresh fruit and tried to organize my unruly thoughts.

"Does your client want you to continue the investigation?" Simon asked.

"Yes," I said. "But I'd do it anyway. This case has become *very* personal."

Simon opened his mouth, his expression suggesting he might be about to issue a parental warning of the need for caution, then apparently he thought better of it. "You will, of course, be careful," he said, with a small ironic smile.

It occurred to me that I didn't know whether Simon had children, or if he'd ever been married. But I thought I'd save that conversation for a day when I might have more time and mind to be present.

Simon excused himself, and I took the opportunity to try to lay out an agenda for the day, using the pad and pen I'd carried with me from the phone stand. I was so concentrated on the task, I didn't notice that he'd returned with my plateful of waffles until he was standing by my chair.

I looked up, a little startled, and stared into his clear blue eyes, a memory hitting me with the force of a fist. The waitress at The Blue Heron. Those bright blue eyes. And her stare: not in irritation that I hadn't noticed her, but because of the letters. I was sitting there reading Alice's letters, laid out as though for all the world to see, and there she was, having to watch.

"What is it?" Simon said. "Pardon the cliché, but you look as though you'd seen a ghost."

I put my hands to my cheeks, which were flushed with heat. "Oh, God," I said, "I think I have.

"Stupid!" I yelled then, banging my fist on the table. "Stupid, stupid, stupid! She was right there, right beside me, I'm sure of it. And I was so wrapped up in the letters—*her* letters—I couldn't even see her."

Simon sat down beside me and I filled him in on my realization. "Those eyes! Just like Mary Alice's. The whole family, in fact. It had to be her. If I'd just realized— But no, I was so wrapped up in my own Miss Marple routine . . ."

Simon put his hand on my arm. "Beating yourself up isn't going to help," he said. "What does it tell you? What new information does this give you that you can use?"

I tried to think. It all seemed so much too little, too late. "She must have followed me," I said finally. "Maybe he'd already targeted her and followed her to the woods. But how? This little caravan of cars to Shepherd's Woods? Without my noticing?" I made a harsh, scoffing sound. "But then, I wasn't exactly noticing much, was I?"

Simon gave my arm a tighter squeeze.

"Okay," I said, "concentrate. Maybe she wanted to speak to me, but not in public like at the café. Maybe she followed Mary Alice to my office, so she knew— But she couldn't have; she was working. She must have taken a waitress job there, at The Blue Heron, after she got dropped from The Queen's Rest for not being classy enough. The Heron's in Grace, where the family lives."

I looked at Simon, wanting him to give me the answers, like a failed contestant on a quiz show.

"Eat," he said. "And we'll try to lay out the variables."

He went to his study and brought back the manila envelope of documents, a white legal pad, and an expensive-looking gray Parker ink pen, which he set before him at his usual place at the other end of the table.

"Assumptions," I said, as though prompted. "I guess the first is that I now believe my case is linked to the Crucifixer somehow. And second, I don't know how."

"Reexamine," Simon said.

I frowned. I really wasn't in the mood for ABCs.

"I'm assuming Alice was in Shepherd's Woods because I live there. That she probably followed me there that first evening. Or maybe found out where I lived and went the next morning. And he followed her."

"Or?"

"Don't go schoolteacher on me, Simon. If you have a point, make it."

"What if he was already in the woods, looking for a victim?"

"And saw her when? She didn't even make contact with me that first night; maybe she was just checking me out, like she did Mary Alice. Or maybe she didn't come till the next day. So who got there first, him or her?"

I wiped a dribble of maple syrup from my chin with the fine linen napkin. I always wanted to ask for paper instead when I came but thought it might be gauche. "Except," I said, "that it must have been them, him and her—or at least him—I saw in the cabin that next morning on my run."

"Had the victim been tortured? Is that why she might have been held before being killed? If indeed he took her that first night."

"The officers who spoke to me at the hospital raised the possibility. But Belgium didn't mention it in the message he left. Just the name."

"Then let's say it was you he had his eye on."

"Let's not," I said darkly.

Simon ignored the remark. "That still leaves the question of any connection to your case. If he came to the woods looking for a solitary victim and spotted you, maybe on your run when you saw movement in the cabin, then followed you to your . . . domicile, you might have been gone by the time he was ready to strike, but he found her there and took her instead. Which would not necessarily make any connection to the case, except as it put her there at the time."

"I feel it in my gut," I said, pushing back the plate with the remaining waffle. "There's a connection. A direct connection."

"Well, never ignore the gut," Simon said lightly.

"If so," I said, "that makes a pretty small pool of

killers to pick from. And most likely makes it a copycat killing, though the police don't think it was. Even the gasoline had been used before."

"So is it with or without the knowledge of law enforcement that you intend to continue your search?"

"Without. At least for now. The paper trail from those registration certificates seems to be leading somewhere, and I want some lead time to pursue it before anybody else makes the connection between Alice and her father. Stepfather. Or whoever."

"Then you haven't told the police anything about your case?"

"No. And I don't intend to until I've followed what evidence I already have. If there's a killer among the principals, I don't want him—or her, I suppose—warned off by any big public investigation."

"Mmmm," Simon murmured. "Let's assume it is a copycat then, just for the sake of argument. That it was your Alice this person wanted to kill, hoping to camouflage the act by killing her in the style of the Crucifixer."

His voice and demeanor were calm, and it occurred to me that I'd never seen Simon express any strong emotion. He seemed entirely ruled by his intellect, which kept everything else under control. True, I hadn't known him long or been with him when he was under any sort of personal stress. Still, to someone who basically wears her heart on her sleeve, it seemed strange. I envied the control but found myself hoping there were still things that moved him—to anger, fear, passion—but at least moved him.

He took up his pen again. "If Ms. Abbott was the intended victim then, what family members would you think might be capable of the crime?"

"Physically or emotionally?"

"Either or both. Let's not rule out anyone who conceivably could have staged the murder—with help if the person physically couldn't have managed it alone."

"Well, just about everyone then, I suppose. There was apparently no love lost between Alice and her mother. And Shirleen's an iron fist in a velvet glove if ever I saw one. Alice calls her a 'jealous bitch' in her letter. Apparently she knew—or at least suspected—what her husband was doing to her daughter. And I guess she chose him. Then kicked him out, too, it looks like."

He wrote the name on his pad. "And the uncle?"

"He seems devoted to Mary Alice, but maybe it was different with the older girl. They would have been much closer in age, only ten or eleven years apart, so they'd have been more like siblings. Maybe there was rivalry.

"God, even Mary Alice herself, I suppose," I said, then immediately felt disloyal to my client. "I have a hard time picturing her doing anything that brutal, but I guess it's the repressed ones who are more likely to snap. Though I can't imagine what the motive would be."

I couldn't sit still another minute. With all the food in me I couldn't possibly do a run, but my limbs needed exercise, so I put them through a series of yoga stretches while we talked.

"The husband's still Suspect Number One though," I said, lunging first over my right bent knee, then the left. "Besides whatever happened with Alice, there's something strange going on there. Mary Alice scarcely remembers him, she was so young when he left. But this thing with the trucks—the papers indicate they were bought *two years* after he supposedly left the home. It makes me wonder just how far out of the picture he's been. And that woman yesterday was truly frightened when I mentioned his name."

I clasped my hands behind my knees and bent forward stiff-legged until my head touched the carpet. My voice came out a little strangled. "I found another address I'm going to check out. On a lease agreement in the cab of a truck at that old I.R.S. address for Harley."

I dropped facedown on the carpet and bent my torso back into the cobra position, catching a glimpse of Simon's amused smile as my head passed up and back as far as it would go. I ignored the smile.

"On the other hand," Simon said, "if the killing is a copycat, the killer wouldn't necessarily have been in the area long. Alice says she was sent away 'for good,' and that she's 'come back,' both of which suggest some distance and that she hasn't been back before. Maybe the killer followed the girl here."

I straightened my head from its backward thrust and looked at him. "Ergo," I said, "the killer could be the biological father. Alice's birth certificate is from a Salt Lake City hospital, and the school said that's where she was sent, to 'her father.' "

"Though in her letter," Simon said, "she refers to a woman, who read the Bible and damned her to hell."

"Maybe his wife at the time, or somebody he dumped her on when he found he couldn't handle her either. Or maybe . . ." I scrambled to my feet. "In those pictures in the hatbox in Shirleen's closet? There were several taken before the parents died, showing them and the two children and some woman in a white uniform. I took her to be the nanny. Maybe she went to Utah when the parents died and took the children with her. And they returned to the island only after they were grown. Maybe that's the woman Shirleen sent Alice to, her own nanny!

"A lot of maybe's, huh?" I said to Simon's less-than-enthusiastic expression. "Besides, from the look of her then, she'd be long dead by now."

"Everything is worth considering," Simon said evenly. "But in such a scenario, are we to assume the father is fiction?"

"Could be," I said. "Shirleen is real attached to appearances; maybe she just refers to him now and then to keep them up. Alice's birth certificate says *Father Unknown*. Maybe Shirleen got around a lot as a teen and doesn't know which one knocked her up." I began gathering the paperwork together. "In any case, once I finish in Seattle I think I'd better make a little trip to Utah, see if there's any trail there that's not stone cold."

"Perhaps I could help in that regard," Simon said, the hesitancy of his tone suggesting that he didn't want to insult my lone-wolf abilities. "I have a colleague in Park City. He's on a retainer to an accident-prone mogul and gets bored in the intervals between. If you wish I could send him the information from the birth certificate. Perhaps he could try to track the father from there."

"That'd be great," I said. "I've got plenty to do here, and I don't know how long it'll take." I looked at my watch; it read just after eight. "And I'd best be getting to it. Thanks so much for everything, Simon. It really helps to be able to talk things out. Not to mention divine food and sleep."

"Did you want to use the SCOIS before you go?" Simon asked, referring to the computer data base he subscribes to that accesses all the court records from Olympia to Emerald, from the local on up to superior-court levels. It does not include information from Prince Island, but I could pursue that when I returned.

We went into Simon's study and he logged on, to the tune of a whole volley of electronic bells and whistles.

The first name I keyed in was Harley Abbott. Though I assumed the marriage had taken place on the island, maybe the divorce had not and might show up in the King County records. But I found neither marriage nor divorce records for the name. Or for Shirleen Holman Abbott Holman.

I had more luck in traffic court. Harley had a string of DUIs from '73 to '79, bringing about a suspended license in both '77 and '78 and finally a loss of license in '79. No wonder he'd had to sell or lease out his trucks, I thought, and keyed in Carl Erchak.

But there was nothing under that name in any of the data bases. Maybe leases weren't recorded, I thought, although the paperwork was in the cab. Or maybe just not that far back. I wasn't surprised, therefore, not to find the name of Roman Marcello in the system either. In fact, I felt a bit relieved: What if the hard-earned information of the day before had been available from such an easy, sterile source?

Not that the information had proved valuable yet; but where would be the feeling of accomplishment if it did? The truth was, if I'd wanted to be a computer desk jockey, that's probably what I'd have done. More money and more safety both, for sure. But there has always seemed something unsporting about tracking a suspect by computer. I mean, can you see Sherlock's steely gaze fixed on a computer screen hour after hour while it made his deductions for him? I've always been most comfortable in motion, and my feet were itching to hit the road again.

CHAPTER 21

THAT MORNING, ROLLING UP I-5 from Olympia to Seattle, the air was soft with spring, the light a tender, nearly iridescent green, as though reflected from all the bits of new growth it could find in the cityscape. I was torn between the call to duty and a desire to just take an off-ramp and head for the wildlife refuge at Ruby Beach or northwest to the dewy virgin forests of the Olympic Peninsula—wherever Nature predominated.

Naturally, duty won; it usually does. But I did make some soon-as-this-is-over promises to myself, which included more time with Gray and with the great outdoors, preferably together. And I stopped off at the Pike Street open-air market for some fresh fruit and veggies to get me through the day without more fat or starch to stretch my jeans to another rip.

The address I had for Roman Marcello proved to be in a light-industrial area within clear hearing distance of the Sea-Tac Airport. I even found the number, though the structure it was attached to looked unpromising: a one-story rectangle about the size of a single-wide mobile home, its sides in bad need of paint and its few windows blanketed from the inside, giving no sign of occupancy.

There was no door on the side facing the street, so I worked my way around the building clockwise, finding none on the end, either, until I turned the corner and encountered a concrete expanse about the size of a basketball court. On the far side, gleaming in the sun, were a sleek black motorcycle, a spanking-new-looking red Ford pickup, and a huge cab that looked a dead ringer for the one at Erchak's. Even the grille seemed to be giving me that same sinister leer, and I felt no desire to get closer. It was clear that I would have to though, because the vanity plate on the pickup read ROMANS.

Two polished black cowboy boots stuck out from beneath the cab, their silver tips shining like chrome. One pointed skyward on the end of an extended leg, the other stood flat below a raised knee, and both rested on what looked to be a large black garbage bag. To keep them from getting scuffed by the concrete?

I bit the bullet and approached. My sneaker steps apparently proved inaudible, so when I'd come as close as I was willing to, I cleared my throat, wondering even as I did so why the human animal has chosen that sound to announce itself.

The boots moved then, and there was the sound of metal wheels rolling on concrete as the black-jeaned legs appeared, followed by a denim work shirt, and finally a head, revealing the somewhat older but no less handsome face of the man in the photograph: Harley Abbott.

I suspect my mouth must have been hanging open for a while before I said, like an idiot, "You're Harley Abbott."

"Among other things," the face said, its sensuous mouth curling in a smile, amusement also in the midnight-blue eyes, topped by smooth brows beneath a crop of thick black curls.

He must get a lot of this reaction, I thought, closing my mouth firmly. Even if the woman isn't caught by surprise.

He rose without using his hands and proceeded to strip off the work shirt to reveal a pristine white T-shirt underneath, its sleeves rolled just above biceps that looked to be less the products of workaholism than hours at the gym.

"I was expecting someone else," I said, as though that would fully explain my confusion. "Is Roman Marcello you too?"

The eyebrows lifted slightly in lazy interest, the smile unmoved. "The girl is clever," he said. Then, reading off the sweatshirt: "University of Chicago. Aren't you a little far from home?"

The reduction to youth status wasn't lost on me. "I was hired by Mary Alice Abbott to find her sister. Alice," I said.

"Ah, Alice," the man said. "Is she missing?"

"She's dead," I said, watching closely for his reaction.

There was almost none. His features seemed fluid for a moment, like a swimmer's look just before he breaks water, the dark eyes unreadable. Then he nodded, barely perceptibly. "I guess I'm not surprised," he said. "The girl was always hell-bent for destruction." Then the cocky grin returned. "It's probably why we got along so well."

"You have any idea who her father was?" I asked, hoping to relax any guard he had up against self-disclosure by aiming at someone else.

"Shirleen said he was a fly-boy from the base, all set to marry her when he went down in flames. But who knows? The woman could romanticize the phone book."

He pivoted then and headed for the building. "What a beer?" he said over his shoulder.

I fell into step behind him, though I had no intention of following him into an enclosed space. I recalled Simon's last words to me that morning, after I confessed that I had left my gun at home: "If you find out where Abbott is, don't go there alone. Call me; I'll go with you."

A little late for that, but at least I paused at the doorstep, and when he held the screen door for me, shook my head.

The grin widened. "The little lady's afraid to be alone with me? Hey, they do say I'm dangerous, but you might find you like it."

I fought against the impulse to show him I was not afraid, but in the end made my better sense rule. "I'll just wait here," I said, as casually as I could fake it.

He shrugged. "Suit yourself," and let the screen door bang behind him as he pushed through the solid door, which he left open.

I was grateful for the intermission and tried to use the time to take stock of my thoughts and formulate the questions I ought to ask.

When he reappeared with the beer, though, and handed me mine, his smile was so seductively self-satisfied that I was annoyed enough to say, "So. Did you have sex with Alice?"

The eyebrows really shot up this time; then he broke into a laugh, displaying perfect white teeth. "Don't be shy now," he said, "just come right out with it."

I pressed the advantage. "Did you?"

"Now, who told you that?"

"I'm an investigator," I said, and left it at that.

"You got some kind of identification?"

I figured he was stalling for time, but I plucked out my photo ID from a zippered pocket in my bag and held it up for his inspection.

He closed his hand over mine, on the pretext of adjusting the card for better viewing. By the time he said, "Doesn't do you justice," he had recovered his cool. "You're a much tastier little morsel in person."

Then he tried to take control of the exchange. "Are you the one went by the Erchak place yesterday? Is that how you got this address; that wife of his give it to you?"

" 'That wife' wouldn't so much as open the door," I said, wanting to make sure she wouldn't get heat from my little escapade.

He stood waiting for me to go on, but I didn't. "My question first," I said.

"What question is that?"

"Cut the crap. You know the question." My fear was diminishing in proportion to my increasing irritation—a fact, I was aware, that might not necessarily work in my favor.

He seemed to take it as his advantage and lounged back against the building in his skintight jeans, one shiny boot crossed over the other. "Did I do the daughter, the pint-size detective wants to know."

He broke off eye contact, and we both waited several moments in silence before he said, "Sure, why not? The kid was no kin of mine, and she was begging for it. A real nympho, just like her mother."

I bit my lip to keep from responding to the label, said instead, "And how did 'her mother' feel about that?"

He shrugged. "Nothing, long as she didn't know. I like sugar, but not at the expense of bread and butter."

"How about bread and water? Alice was still a minor."

He just grinned. "Nothing minor about Alice. She could toss ass with the best of 'em."

"So you're claiming it was consensual. With a sixteen-year-old girl. Right under her mother's roof."

A ripple of something flitted across his face. Confusion? Guilt? Had he started on her when she was younger, as she suspected?

Then it was gone, replaced by the same lazy, sexy grin I was beginning to hate. "No risk, no spice," he said.

"For Alice or you?"

"Oh, Alice loved her spice. *Especially* under her mother's roof."

I was dearly wanting to knock him off balance again. "Then how about your own daughter? When did you introduce spice into *her* diet?"

"My own—Mary? That Plain Jane, *my* blood?!" He laughed harshly. "She was already a rug rat when I entered the picture and not much more than that when I left."

Inside, a phone rang.

Harley's cocky grin deepened in both dimples, and he pushed himself upright. "You'll have to excuse me," he said, and swiveled his tight butt toward the door.

This time my curiosity about the interior of the place overcame my caution, and when I heard Harley engaged in what sounded like an extended conversation, I went in too.

The place was depressingly shabby: a narrow rectangular room with a scarred desk across from the door, under a window shaded with yellowing canvas.

Harley sat perched on a corner of the desk talking on the phone, his back to me. He turned around when

I entered and frowned, lowering his voice, although all he was saying was, "Yeah? When?" and "Two or three?"

My gaze lit covetously on a battered black two-drawer file cabinet at the far end of the room. A lock had been welded into the frame more recently. But maybe it was pickable. I may have left my gun at home, but I always carry my picks. That had been high on my list when I became a P.I.: Learn how to pick locks. It's no more legal for P.I.s than for the police, but there's less likely to be somebody looking over your shoulder.

At the other end of the room hung a drape—red cotton, in need of a wash. If Harley lived in this place it would have to be in the section beyond the drape, which could not be big. I couldn't see the man bringing his conquests back to such sorry digs; maybe this was just an office and he lived elsewhere. Under what name, I wondered.

Then it occurred to me to go have a closer look at that motorcycle, and I passed back through the screen door and approached the trio of gleaming vehicles, thinking disparaging thoughts about men and their love affairs with anything on wheels.

My hunch was confirmed: The motorcycle was a Harley-Davidson. Five would get you ten that Harley Abbott was an alias as well, probably one in a lengthy chain forged to evade authorities of various sorts, including those bearing subpoenas in paternity suits. Prince Island can be a magnet for such escapees from the law.

I could hear Harley/Roman/Whoever coming up behind me, his boots tapping authoritatively along the concrete. I didn't turn; I didn't want him to think I had any fear of him.

He circled me and mounted the motorcycle, having added a black leather aviator's jacket, helmet, and gloves to his outfit.

"Why Abbott?" I said, just as he was raising himself to come down on the starter pedal.

There was real irritation in his smile this time; I was pushing it with the questions.

"First name in the yellow-pages listings," he said, then stomped the motor to life, making me instinctively fall back a step.

He said something I couldn't hear over the roar.

"What?" I yelled.

He repeated it, no louder, forcing me to approach—all part of his game.

I sauntered forward as coolly as I knew how, until he was much too close for comfort, the opaque smoked plastic of his goggles making the term *Hell's Angels* leap to mind.

"It's been fun," he said, though his mouth wasn't smiling. "But this is where it ends. No more sneaking around and poking your nose where it doesn't belong. Because next time I might get angry. And you wouldn't like me when I'm angry." Then he peeled rubber across the concrete and was gone.

I stood there thinking, this man must not take me too seriously if he feels free to leave me here with whatever secrets lie inside that building only a door or window away. Unless, of course, he is setting a trap, hoping to catch me in the act, and will be rolling back here in ten minutes. Or he considers his security here unbreachable; an alarm system maybe?

But gazing at the rundown place, it seemed unlikely. A man that cocky tends to consider himself invulnerable, especially to women, I told myself. And never let it be said that I missed a chance to break and enter.

As a formality, I tested the doorknob, though I knew Harley wasn't going to let me near that file cabinet. But the knob-mounted lock picked easily.

I headed first for the red drape to check out what I presumed to be the bedroom. I saw only a bare double mattress along the front wall, with an old yellow blanket twisted across it, two striped caseless pillows at its head. I opened the one small closet but found only piles of used clothing inside, including a few shapeless jackets that were definitely not the man's style.

It was seeming less and less likely that this was the impeccable Harley's crash pad at all, but I didn't have time to reflect on the subject; I didn't know when he'd return. I pushed back through the red drape to the office room and made for the file.

The cabinet was indeed locked, and on closer inspection, the hefty metal looked unpickable. But it didn't take long to locate the key. Most people are lazy: They'll drive up and down the aisles for ten minutes just to find the closest possible parking space to the store they want to enter. And at least half the population hides the copy of their door key either under the mat or on the top ledge of the frame.

I noticed that the file cabinet was not flush with the wall and felt behind it. There, about two inches below the surface, I felt a nail driven into the wall, and on the nail a key.

I didn't stay long with any one file. I had nearly been caught twice so far in this investigation and felt really opposed to making it three. I entertained a brief but dismal picture of hiding under all the soiled clothing in the bedroom closet, just waiting for Harley to step on me.

In the top drawer were dog-eared folders with labels stuck one on top of another on their tabs. The latest labels seemed to be written in code: KKLN, OCHEM, BLS. Inside were copies of receipts from the kind of simple invoice pad you can buy in most any discount store. They were dated in the upper right-hand corner, the *To* line carrying the code, the *From* line containing only initials. RM, CE, and FD were the ones I saw in a quick scan.

Nothing was written on the lines for listing the contents of the transaction, only a four- to six-figure dollar amount in the price column. There were also no signatures of buyer or seller, though each was marked *Paid* diagonally across it. All the receipts seemed to be made out by the same hand, as were the *Paid* markers; only the initials appeared differently styled.

I pulled a sample from each folder and moved down to the lower drawer. Piles of empty folders stood in front, behind them a stack of license plates, both new and used.

I pulled out the plates. They looked to be of two sorts: those marked TRACTOR or TRAILER PRIVATE across the top, above the usual assortment of letters and numbers; and those I took for use on the more personal vehicles, a collection of vanity plates reading STUD 1, PRIMO, AMOROSO, etc. If these were all referents to the driver, I thought, they certainly were monothematic.

I crossed to the desk in search of paper and pen to write them down and made my greatest discovery in its single drawer: a legal pad with a whole string of names on it, with practice signatures after each. From the kinship of both names and signatures, my guess was that they were all aliases for the man I knew as Harley Abbott.

I tore off the sheet, jotted down the license plates

and the acronyms for the customers on another, and stuffed both into the pocket of my jeans, putting everything back in its respective drawer. Then I locked the cabinet and returned the key to its nail. Twenty-two minutes, my watch said: past time to be out of there.

The guardian angel of reckless P.I.s was on the job though. I peeked out the front door and saw no one on the street, so I slipped outside, set the lock and pulled the door shut behind me, and walked back to my car at a studiously casual pace. An altogether clean getaway.

CHAPTER 22

I HEADED FOR THE MAIN BRANCH of the library on 4th Avenue to see whether their collection of phone directories went back far enough to put some dates with Harley's aliases and give an idea of who and where the man was when.

Before heading for the Reference section though, I gave Gray a call from one of the pay phones in the foyer. It looked to me as though I had a full afternoon's work ahead of me, and I thought I might stay with him that night before returning to the island. Missing Sunday had made the week feel incomplete—not to mention myself.

I felt more thankful than ever for our pact not to speak of our ongoing cases. He'd have no way of knowing that the Crucifixer's island victim had been the object of my own search, and therefore wouldn't feel compelled to argue me out of keeping on the case.

Gray was at his desk.

"Hey, babe."

"Molly. Which continent are you on?"

Gray maintained that anything west of Washington's shores was another country. I kept hoping he was right.

"City of Seattle," I said.

"How's your head?"

"Still got it. Not as big a headache as my case though."

"What's up?"

"Against the rules, babe. Looks like it's going to tie me up all day, though, in research. What are you doing tonight?"

"I've got duty till nine. After that, I'm all yours."

"Promises, promises." He wasn't the only one who worried in this relationship. Chief of Police, even in Sleepytown, U.S.A., isn't exactly a vacation anymore.

"They identified your Crucifixer victim," he said, in that controlled tone of voice that suggested he'd rather not bring up the subject at all. Like I'd forget?

"Yeah," I said, "Belgium left a message on my machine. Just the name though. Said they got it from old juvy records. Have they found anything else of significance?"

"Not much. Seems she's been living in Utah, according to the mother, just came back for a visit with the family."

"Helluva welcome," I said, imagining the bosom-of-the-family tale Shirleen must have concocted.

"Speaking of which, your mother called last night."

Oops. My parents thought I was living full time with Gray in Emerald. Another fiancé dodge. I didn't like the deception but liked their worrying even less. It didn't play, ethically, but it was the best I could do. My parents had had me late in life, and I was their only child. In a way they were like grandparents to me, including the spoiling of the only grandkid. I loved them to pieces, but I needed to keep some distance between us to feel fully grown. When you look in the mirror and I'm what you see, it's a little easier to be persuaded you are still among the young'uns.

"I'll call them," I said. "While I wait for you. Be careful, okay?"

"You too."

"I will."

Who did we think we were fooling?

I seated myself at a long table in the Reference section and pulled out my list of aliases. My, my, my, I thought as I scanned it, haven't we been a busy—and changeable—boy.

I hauled out the phone books for Seattle and Island County all the way back to five years before the marriage of Shirleen and Harley. None of the aliases appeared in either location for the first four. Then a listing in the Island yellow pages showed up the year before the marriage, a one-liner for *Abbott's Fix-It* under *Automobile Repair & Service*, with a Port Angel address.

The next year, which would have been the year of the marriage, the outfit had a two-column display ad, Harley's name in eighteen-point boldface, and included *Trucking Services* among its specialties.

The ad reappeared the next year, but the third year after the marriage, the listings disappeared in Island County but began in the Seattle yellow pages—a one-inch box under *Trucking–Hauling*, listing only *Special Services* as the nebulous offering. There was Harley's name, a phone number, and the address of the jumbo-size garage where the Erchaks now resided. No wonder Mary Alice didn't remember Harley, I thought: He'd stayed only two years in the marriage; she wouldn't even have been three yet.

The original Seattle ad appeared for one year only;

then the aliases began cropping up, with phone numbers but no addresses, under the same *Trucking–Hauling* head. *Special Services* was the only text, and the names kept changing, from Abbott to Mark Davidson (the other half of the Harley?), to Tony Navaronne, to Julius D'Amato, to Anthony Amoroso. . . . Each one appeared for one to three years, then changed, including the phone number. This was the second year for Roman Marcello.

You didn't have to be Sherlock to figure out that these "special services" might involve something less than legal. I copied down all the names and numbers, though I didn't know just what I'd do with the information. Probably the I.R.S. would be happy to have it; none of these after-Abbott guys were likely to have paid their taxes. And there was likely a forger in the wings, supplying Chameleon Harley with new IDs as he went along. That would make at least three currently involved in the scam, if you counted Erchak.

Erchak. Maybe, I thought, my pen poised between my teeth . . . Maybe poor Mrs. Erchak's fear of me was that of an illegal alien for any citizen who might come knocking at the door. Illegals smuggled in would make a very obedient work force. I thought of the shabby building I'd just left, its piles of dirty, overworn clothing. A way station for illegal immigrants? Add the Immigration Service to the list of potentially interested parties.

My own interest, though, was more in the man's personal proclivities and whether they had led him beyond scams to murder and more. I'd had enough of research and returned the books to their shelves. It was now 3:40; I'd stake out the place for two hours before I headed up to Emerald. If the Crucifixer's madness was accelerating, and Harley was Suspect Number One, I'd better find out what he was up to out there in the world and what-all he considered his "special services." If his aliases and his vanity plates were any indication, the man was just a tad sex-obsessed. Just how many steps were there from superstud to sadistic killer?

Before I left the library, I detoured through the Social Sciences section and selected a title from their alarming number of shelves on multiple murders. Wanting something that might give local examples, I chose *The Who and Why of Serial Killers,* written by a University of Washington professor—a little light reading to fend off stakeout boredom.

I'd had barely enough time to conceal my car behind an empty van in the neighboring plumbing supplies parking lot before the red pickup came roaring up, doing fifty easy, and jolted onto the concrete pad behind the building.

Both the motorcycle and the cab were gone, and the pickup swung round and backed up to the door of the low building. Harley dropped from the driver's seat and unlocked the door, propping the screen door open with a chunk of wood that stood below it, apparently for the purpose.

He pulled a stack of empty cartons off the bed of the pickup, leaving the gate down, and soon reappeared from the building with the first of them filled, shoved it into the truck bed, and returned to the interior.

I must've been made, I thought, and he's moving the office. But how? I reviewed all my moves in my head and couldn't think where I'd slipped up. Unless the man didn't go far when he left. Maybe he'd only roared off on the motorcycle and parked it down the street, then came back on foot to see what I was up to. My skin turned clammy and my breath short. Was whatever he was into so illegal that the mere appearance of an investigator was threatening enough to move? Maybe I'd been wrong in my assessment that he'd dismissed me as a woman playing private eye and considered me no threat. But then why hadn't he stopped me at the time?

None of these questions was finding an answer before the man was finished and closed both doors, climbing back into the driver's seat of the pickup.

I couldn't not follow him. I stayed as far back as I could and still keep the pickup in sight, putting two or three vehicles between us at all times. If he was keeping an eye on the rearview mirror, it didn't seem to hinder his progress, and he made no evasive moves onto side streets or by changing speed. The pickup barreled down the highway at the same good clip until it swung off into the parking lot of the Blue Moon Motel, where it parked against the fence separating the motel from Hoppy's Short-Stop Diner.

I turned the corner and pulled into the diner's lot, behind a line of vehicles parked at the fence, and watched from between a blue Pontiac and a dirty white Voyager as Harley dismounted and strode toward the motel.

He didn't head for the office but climbed a flight of stairs on the rear flank of the pink adobe two-story to a door marked 18 and entered with a key.

I waited for a moment, undecided what to do. The motel lot was virtually empty of cars at that hour, and I'd stand out like a passerby crossing a firing range. But what were my options?

I parked the Honda at the rear of the diner's lot and doubled back. The motel building was *L*-shape, with the office at the juncture of the legs. I circled to the end of the longer section, then clung close to the sides of the building so I couldn't be spotted from above. Once I reached the stairs, though, tacked to the building like a fire escape, there was nothing for it but to climb them. I took a deep breath and shot up the staircase two at a time, then flattened myself against the door of Room 24 at their top. Which was ludicrous, of course, since the doors were flush with the walls, and anyone coming out of any door along that entire side of the building could have seen me clearly.

Still, I'd gotten myself into this, so I figured I might as well do what I came for.

I crept to Room 18 and tried to peer through the drapes. The folds covered the window on the near side and overlapped at the center, but I discovered a small gap on the far side through which I could see most of the room, including the bed.

What I saw made me gasp out loud and set my mind racing for ways to intervene. Harley Abbott, undisguised by a black Zorro-style mask over his eyes, held his ex-wife by the throat with his left hand, while his right pulled the pins from her chignon until her blond hair rippled to her shoulders.

Moving his left hand to grip her hair, he pulled her head back and fastened his mouth on hers in a kiss too rough to have sprung from affection, then lifted her, hands clamped on her breasts, and flung her on the bed.

Shirleen squirmed and gave little cries, her eyes closed, while he tore her sky-blue silk dress down the front, seams ripping, and threw it back to reveal lingerie that would make Fredericks of Hollywood look classy.

Somewhere along the way I stopped trying to figure out how to get in and immobilize Harley without my gun. For one thing, I noticed that there were already handcuffs attached to the bedposts and a whip propped against the wall by the bed—none of which Harley could have brought in with him. They must either remain in the room or were brought there by Shirleen, who apparently had arrived before us. For another, the woman's histrionics, thrashing and moaning as the cuffs were snapped over her wrists, were so melodramatic and *un*-self-protective, I concluded that this was just a regular afternoon pastime for the two, who clearly kept themselves in excellent shape for their roles, as though a photographer for pulp paperbacks might burst in at any moment with flashbulbs popping.

Harley stood on the bed shedding his own clothes, while Shirleen's small bare feet passed over his body like caressing hands, until he was stripped down to a shiny black bikini and his cowboy boots.

Then his lips pulled back in a snarl below the mask, white teeth gleaming, as he bent to grasp Shirleen's ankles, pulling her legs apart to the full extension of his arms, and stomped one bootheel into her crotch with a force that had to hurt.

My sense of alarm returned, not only because of the brutality of the act, but because when Harley bent forward there had swung from around his neck, on a thin gold chain, the figure of a crucifix.

This time I could hear Shirleen's cries through the closed window. But her expression did not change to one of fear or anger; only a trembling began in her body that increased steadily as Harley grabbed up the whip and proceeded to crack it, over and over, just short of her flesh, until finally he pushed down his bikini and threatened her with his own blunt instrument.

I was trembling some myself as I backed away

from the window and retraced my steps to my car. Was this really nothing but the sick game it appeared to be, a sadomasochistic therapy session between a jerk who'd perfected the role of the bad boy and a control freak desperate to let go? Or had one or both of them lost control and pushed fantasy into reality?

Either way the scene had knocked me down a well of murky depression. Was this the sort of sex Harley had laid on the young Alice? Something she would later refuse to do even for survival on the streets?

And bottom line, just when had sex gotten to be so much about power and so little about love?

CHAPTER 23

I SAT IN MY LOCKED CAR, windows rolled up, stewing in the trapped heat of the spring sunshine, and wondered glumly what new information this little episode had left me with. Clearly, there were ties still unsevered between Shirleen and her ex. But did they go beyond sick sex? Was she maybe bankrolling his extralegal activities, whatever they were? In exchange for what, a cut of the take and afternoons of twisted passion?

And what about him? Was Harley the Crucifixer or just an aging adolescent still in love with his own powers to thrill or humiliate? Which might also be components of the psyche of the Crucifixer, I reminded myself. Although he could have just copycatted for the occasion.

So where was that *aha!* feeling I usually get when a puzzle has been solved? What more did I want? There was connection, even accusation, motive if Alice's return would have blown his little deal with his ex. Maybe he made house calls, too, and had spotted Alice lurking about the grounds, thought he'd better see to it that she didn't overturn the golden applecart.

I didn't have long to ponder the question before the door to Room 18 opened and Shirleen slipped through it, looking furtively left and right like a cat burglar.

"I'm right here, honey," I said aloud from the shelter of my car, "and I saw all your dirty laundry."

My smugness was short-lived, however, as the woman hustled to the end of the fencing on the far side and rounded it into the diner's parking lot, where I was sitting. Does she know my car? I asked myself. I'd parked around the corner when I'd searched the house, but it was right out front the evening of the dinner. Wendell would have seen it, since he arrived after me, but had she? Had the little scene with the bandage made her suspicious enough to peer out the window and and watch me drive off? Worse, I realized that I wouldn't recognize her car either; it must have been in the closed garage that evening.

In any event it was too late now; starting the motor would only call more attention to my car. I slumped in the seat as she approached, though I couldn't quite make myself sink so low that I'd be entirely unable to see her. It would feel too much like making myself the proverbial fish in the barrel.

The afternoon sun was halfway down the western sky, putting it right in her eyes. Shirleen shaded them with her left hand, her right gripping a needlepoint bag large enough to hold the torn blue dress. I wondered what—if anything—she was still wearing, then, under her stylish pale tan trench coat.

When she reached the corner of the diner, though, she turned left; apparently her car was parked on the other side. I sat up, waiting until I heard a motor start, then got out and slipped from car to car until I could see around the back of the diner, where a white Lincoln convertible whipped out of the drive and turned north.

I figured Shirleen was headed home to play the pious mother, and I went back to my car to wait for Harley to emerge. It was a short wait, and he looked like a man in a hurry, his boots tapping a staccato beat down the stairs and striding to his truck, looking neither left nor right.

I started my motor and cruised to the edge of the diner's driveway, until I saw the red pickup swing onto the street and turn east.

Wherever he was going, he was going there fast. I had to do sixty in the stretches to keep up with him and almost lost him twice, expecting any minute to hear a police siren and get pulled over for speeding while he got away clean.

The landscape gradually changed from fast-food joints and gas stations to residential streets with an occasional corner grocery. I had to be more careful here, since the traffic was lighter. There was nothing between us at one point, and I turned into a private drive, waiting until I saw him hang a right two blocks ahead before I backed out and chased after him again.

By the time the truck stopped, we were in the working-class suburb of Blakesly. I drove on past the driveway Harley had turned into but couldn't help slowing and rubbernecking at the sight. Beyond a parking lot and playing field, a low, sprawling building, identified by a sign as Blakesly Elementary, was almost entirely swathed in gauzy white. And milling about it were figures also encased in bulky white jumpsuits, wearing helmets and gas masks, walking about stiff-legged on plastic-bootied feet. I felt as if I'd stepped into an episode of *The X-Files*.

I drove as slowly as I dared to the corner and looked left and right for a place where I might observe whatever was going on without being observed myself.

Halfway down the block to my right, three rigs such as the one I'd seen in the outsize Erchak garage were parked in a church's lot, and in all three, drivers sat at the wheels.

I drove quickly across the street and into the next block, though as far as I knew, none of those drivers had ever had occasion to see my car.

I turned left at the next corner and parked in the back of a convenience store, not yet within sight of the school, then rummaged through my garbage bag of sweats in the backseat until I found a pair whose smell I could stand and a sweatband, adding sunglasses for extra identity protection. Then I got out, locked the car, and began jogging down the street toward the school.

It was even eerier from the front. A sign staked into what once was grass read in large red letters:

DANGER
Asbestos Abatement in Progress
Authorized Personnel Only

From the large white circus-style tent that I took to be Command Central for the operation, twenty-some feet of white duct tubing, a good six feet in diameter, led to the rear of the cocooned building. Along its length it was broken in two places by smaller tents, in what I guessed must be a process of progressive decontamination of the workers, since the last few stragglers were now emerging with wet heads and dry civvies and taking off in their cars. Changing of the guard, I figured. Soon only one was left, and he was deep in conversation with Harley, who apparently felt the suit did not measure up to his sense of style, because he still wore the black jeans and white T-shirt I'd seen him in that morning, the ones he'd shed while playing The Bandit and The Slave Girl.

I jogged as slowly as I dared, looking across the street only sideways without turning my head. I was nearly past the school when I spied the three big rigs approaching single file from the rear driveway. I chanced a glance behind me and saw Harley speaking into a cellular phone, while the suited one was gesturing with his arms for the trucks to approach.

The air smelled sharply of chalk dust and moldy canvas, and I had no stomach for a return jog, which would make me too conspicuous in any case. So I turned the corner when I came to it, looking for some access to the rear of the houses along that block.

I found an alley and went down it until I could see the backyard of a house midblock that seemed to afford an unobstructed view of the proceedings across the street.

I ambled along at a casual pace—if someone coming down an alley from the rear can be considered casual. There was a sandbox and two plastic tricycles in the shallow yard but no children in sight. A single-car garage stood open at the rear of the narrow driveway, and no movement was apparent in the house.

I approached the rear door of its screened porch and, finding it unlocked, went in. A door to the right led to the house, and I was about to knock on it when I realized I couldn't think of a single reason for my being there and asking if I could spy on the goings-on across the street through their screen. So I left it to the Fates and waded through piles of plastic blocks, a caved-in raceway, and a wheelless wagon lying crippled on its side to the front screen of the porch.

The first rig was already loaded and the second in place, with its back gate down. Three men—the first one Erchak, judging from his size—stood in a loading line, lifting four-foot-high containers piled with debris from a side door of the school to the man standing on the open rear edge of the box trailer, to another pair of arms that pulled it into the interior of the box.

They were working swiftly, but the man in white still kept looking about with an anxious air, maybe watching for the arrival of the next crew or for a vehicle marked E.P.A. to come barreling down the street and announce that the jig was up. You didn't have to be an expert on asbestos to figure out that all these enshrouded precautions around the removal were not meant to lead to this hefting about of the debris in the open air, to be carried off—to some landfill was my guess—rather than disposed of by the surely more expensive means for which the company must have contracted.

I'd assumed Harley's was the pair of arms in the truck, until I saw him, wearing a gas mask like the overseer's, watching at some distance back from the scene. I probably only imagined that he was looking my way as well. Surely he wouldn't be able to see into the dim screened porch from the sunlight in which he stood. But I retreated anyway, through the door and down the steps from the porch, and backtracked to the alley, following it in the other direction until I came to the rear of the convenience store where my Civic was parked.

I briefly considered following the trucks, once they all were loaded, but decided against it. Wherever they were headed was probably at some distance, most likely over the state border to contaminate somebody else's backyard. A word in the ear of the Environmental Protection Agency would probably serve as well to perform my civic duty in the matter.

Besides, it was doubtful that the well-protected Harley would be accompanying his minions on their contaminating journey. He'd speed off in his rakish red truck, probably to some other rendezvous with some other willing victim. I was past shock and deep into fatigue, wanting only a hot bath and a bed and some loving arms around me. I pulled into the street and headed toward Emerald.

CHAPTER 24

ALL THE WAY TO GRAY'S I fantasized about a steamy tub and a chilly piña colada. (I'd sworn off sexual fantasies for the time being, until I could be reassured that desire was a by-product of something I still stubbornly called love.)

After a quick bite of leftover enchiladas from the refrigerator, I still had hours to wait before Gray would return, so I set my book on the clever stand that spans the tub and read of serial killers while I soaked my body and sipped my drink. Not surprisingly, my mood did not lighten.

The book's author was a PhD'd professor at the University of Washington, who drew most of the examples for his thesis from past serial killings in the state. His prototypical offender was familiar enough: the loner white male with the traumatic childhood, generally including sexual dysfunction that escalated his needs for stimulation. The thesis was not new either: that the driving force was the killer's need to prove himself, over and over, as a potent male, his victims being surrogates for whomever he considered responsible for his twisted development.

What held my interest were the case histories, most

of which I was unfamiliar with as a newcomer to the state. The book was published when I was ten, and many of the killings described took place before I was even born. I was amazed and disheartened to realize how many such multiple, seemingly random killings there had been—so many and for so long that a person from another generation or area of the country might not even have heard of them. An endless and escalating epidemic.

The majority of victims seemed to be from the more vulnerable classes of women—prostitutes and young girls. In one account, more than twenty years ago in Genessee, Washington, only a county away, four victims killed over a period of eight months were girls ranging in age from thirteen to fifteen, all the murders following the same M.O.: The killer entered the girl's room through an open window while she was sleeping and raped her, then strangled her with the ripped cloth of her nightgown. In a travesty of Shakespeare, the killer had been dubbed the Romeo Strangler, apparently because all the girls had been killed in their second-story bedrooms, which could only have been reached by the killer's climbing a tree or trellis.

The book, on top of the sick scenes of the day and the revelation of Alice's death, was depressing me faster than the bath and rum could relax me, so I got out, toweled off, and put on a pair of Gray's flannel PJs, then set myself up in bed and punched the remote to the TV across the room.

It was news that came on, and I was about to switch to something more cheerful when I realized that it was KEM, Wendell's station, and thought it might be interesting to review the man in his weatherman persona now that I'd observed him as uncle/brother.

The studio set was designed with a backdrop behind each person of the news team, representing apparently his or her particular areas of interest. Behind anchor Ken Polson was a map of the world, while photos of state and local dignitaries were arranged in collage behind Chandra Firth, the home-state reporter. When the camera turned to Wendell, at his table off to the side, the Big Guy appeared before a bright array of T-shirts from the area schools he seemed to be forever visiting in a mission to spread meteorological wisdom to the young.

He looked dapper in a navy blazer with gold buttons and smiled broadly for the camera, whether he was telling of the storm to come tomorrow or the pancake breakfast being organized to benefit a local boy in need of a bone marrow transplant. Then I heard Gray come in downstairs and shut it off.

We got off to a shamefully late start the next morning. Having been held all night like a sick child, I was ready for adult desire by morning. We dallied, then slept, then dallied some more. By the time our consciences made themselves heard, it was nearly eleven.

After Gray left I called my client, relieved to find her at work.

"It's easier to be here than home," she said. "There've been so many people over from the church ever since we got the news. Every new person gets Mother going again. We haven't even had a chance to talk. So finally I just went off to work."

There was a briskness, almost a coldness, to Mary Alice's voice that was new, as though the emotional distance between her and her mother had widened in that single day, until now they were virtually out of reach. But there was something else.

"How are *you* doing?" I asked.

"I'm okay," she said, sounding a little surprised. "It's so strange, Molly. I think I've begun to remember things about Alice. I remember our rooms. They were at the back of the house, where it's all closed off now. And I remember how Alice got out when she used to leave at night. There's a tree. I went back and looked at it, like I'd never really seen it before, and it's still there. It goes right up to her window. And Molly, I think I remember something about what she was talking about in her letter, the . . . visits. I remember hearing somebody, a voice, low, in her room, late at night. Lots of nights. Then her crying. I tried to go in once while she was crying, but she told me to go back to my room, to lock the door and stay in my room and not open the door to anybody. I remember her saying that so clearly, like it was yesterday."

It was by far the longest I had ever heard Mary Alice speak, as though with her memories she was reclaiming her voice. And she'd called me Molly, more a contemporary than her hired savior.

"Can you remember at all who it was, the person in her room?"

"Oh, no," she said quickly. "I don't think I know that."

Let it come as it comes, I told myself. "Has your mother said anything about Alice since you heard, about her leaving or anything?"

"No. We're never alone. That's why I figured I might as well go back to work."

Then there were the harder questions.

"Mary Alice," I said, "I have to ask you about some other things. It's routine, you understand, in a situation like this involving family. We have to look at everyone."

"Yes?"

"Last Monday and Tuesday, can you think where your mother and your uncle were on those two days?"

There was silence.

"Remember that Monday was the day you came to see me, and Tuesday was when we went to the restaurant and the post office. Did you see your uncle at all during that time?"

Guardedly, she said, "He was staying with us that weekend, helping Mother with something, something to do with the house. But then he went back to Emerald."

"Are you sure?"

"Well, I was at work before I came to your office. When I got home, though, he'd already left."

"And Tuesday?"

"I didn't see him at all on Tuesday. Except on the news, the TV, that night."

"Are you sure you saw him give the weather that night?"

"Yes. I missed the six o'clock, but he was on the eleven. Mother woke me because they were talking about the killing and she was scared. Uncle Wendell was there at the station, working right along with the rest of them, trying to get the latest information."

"On camera?"

"Sure. The station has been trying to show more on-the-scene kinds of pictures, how the newsroom works, that sort of thing."

"How about your mother? Was she at home both nights?"

"Well, Monday she was. But Tuesday is her Bible class at the church. She doesn't usually get home Tuesdays until after I'm asleep. That's why she'd turned on the news so late, I guess."

I'd thought she didn't watch the news. Hear no evil, see no evil . . .

"When do you usually go to bed?"

"At nine."

"Did you hear her come in?"

"I don't wake up once I'm asleep."

The pills, the ones she'd brought out of Shirleen's bathroom, during our search.

"Is that because of the medication you take? You said the pills were for your nerves, that your mother gets them for you."

"Yes. I haven't had any problem sleeping since then."

"When did you start taking them?"

"Oh, a long time ago. Since I was a child."

There'd been a slight pause before the last word. She'd made the connection too. "Can you remember the exact age?"

"It seems like I've always been given things for my nerves. And to help me sleep. But I think these pills were prescribed by Mother's doctor when I started school. I hated it there. I got sick every day. So they put me on different things to calm me."

No wonder her nighttime memories were limited. I decided to return to the original question. "Does your mother go out regularly on other nights, other than Tuesdays?"

"No, not anymore, not anywhere but church."

"When did that stop, her going out at night, when you said she used to wear the hats?"

"Mmm, about a year ago, I guess. She started believing it was a sin."

"How about Wednesday, before I came to dinner? When did you get home?"

"I left work about three. Lasagna takes a long time."

"Yes, I didn't mean to put you to all that trouble."

"It's nice to cook for somebody else, outside the family. We don't have much company. Until now," she added somewhat bitterly.

"Was your mother at home when you got there?"

"Yes. But when I told her you were coming, she went out to get bread, French bread. You know that place she goes, Pierre's?"

I'd seen Pierre. Another boy toy?

"And your uncle? Had you heard from him before he arrived?"

"He and Mother had a fight the night before on the phone. When we heard about the killing we didn't know it was Alice, of course, but Mother was afraid to be alone there, just with me. She asked Uncle Wendell to come right then, but he said he couldn't leave the station, that he had to stay and be there for the latest news. He said he'd come the next night, Wednesday, which he did. She said we couldn't count on him, though, anymore, that there was probably somebody else he wanted to be with. But I knew that wasn't true. He's always said we're his family, the only one he needs."

So much for Windy Holman as a suspect.

"Okay, thanks, Mary Alice. I'm sorry about all the questions when you've had such a shock. I'm just trying to be thorough. Will you be at work the rest of the day, do you think?"

"Probably. Mother seems to have everyone she needs to comfort her." The bitterness again.

"I'd like to come by, whenever I can get back to the island, and speak to your mother if she's up to it. I'd like you there too."

"Sure. When?"

"Say by four? Could you get away by then?"

"Sure. They didn't really expect me in as it was. And I won't have to stop for groceries; people have brought enough food to last us a week."

"Okay, see you then. Hang in there."

"I will," Mary Alice answered, with that new tinge of certainty to her tone.

Then I called the station, to check Wendell's alibi.

"KEM," said a woman with an upbeat voice.

"I wonder if I could speak with the station manager."

"Mister Elder? I'm afraid he's not in, not until four this afternoon. Could I help you with anything?"

"I hope so. Who am I speaking to?"

"Rachel Kleinman. I'm the administrative assistant for the station."

"Perfect." The A.A. title usually designates the person who really runs things, while the higher echelons get the bucks.

The voice sounded young, so I tried to style my story accordingly. "It's a silly thing, really, but it's gotten kind of important. My boyfriend and I are having this contest about who can remember things the best? And the stakes just jumped big time. Like, if I win it's a weekend at the Seattle Hilton! Or some sports thing if he does. Yuck! So this latest thing is, who did the weather last week? On Tuesday, when that awful murder happened on Prince Island. I say that Windy person did the weather that night, but Peter says it was the other one, that woman."

"Carolyn Walsh."

"Right. You can see why I'm trying to improve my memory!"

"Well, I guess you're both right. Carolyn did the

six o'clock. Windy was supposed to do the ten and eleven o'clock, and he got here right before ten."

"You're sure it was ten?"

"Of course. That night'll be hard to forget. We heard the Crucifixer was back right after the ten o'clock, and everybody was on the phones trying to get all the details by eleven. Windy was making calls too. He has family on the island, I think."

"Wow. Okay, let me ask you another thing. That next Saturday, when that woman was killed in Emerald? Who did the weather then?"

There was a silence. Too many links to the killings.

"That's how I remember things," I added hastily. "I try to connect them to some public event, which is easier to remember." I squinted in pain at my awkwardness and fought the impulse to hang up the phone.

"Actually," she said more coolly, "I don't know about that weekend. My husband and I went camping and didn't get back until Sunday. I was glad to have missed it."

I didn't press the issue, just thanked her and hung up. Maybe I'd go by the station later, try to pin down Wendell's presence that evening. But he did seem to be ruled out as Alice's killer, copycat or otherwise. Even if the woman was off by half an hour, there'd be no way he could have been killing his niece and clobbering me in Shepherd's Woods at shortly after ten and gotten back to Emerald at anything like the same time. The ferry ride alone is twenty minutes, with another fifteen to twenty at each end.

I decided to drop by Wendell's residence and see if we could chat without the presence of his sister to inhibit him. If he was clean, she might not be. Many a soul has set out for Bible school and ended up elsewhere. Like at the Blue Moon Motel? Maybe whips were just foreplay for stakes through the heart. Another common interest between her and her ex?

Skyline Drive, the address I had for Wendell, is just north of Gray's address, where the city meets the suburbs. I had seen the development, Cranberry Cliffs, only from a distance and hoped it would look more inviting at closer range. It didn't.

The cranberry of the title was more like the rust of clay, a whole minimountain of it, and the developers must never have heard of mud slides. What might seem impenetrable if you're trying to hack a garden out of it is still a far cry from granite, and bearing the weight of forty ultramodern edifices is a lot to ask out of a cliff full of clay.

To add recklessness to stupidity, the bluff had been hacked into terraces, with all houses facing west so each tenant would have that ever-popular waterfront view of Possession Sound. And from the road each house looked to be built to the very edge of its designated perch, in a kind of architectural brinkmanship.

Closer up they looked even more precarious, each house poised on the edge of its terrace like a brazen child standing as close as he can to whatever brink his parent has warned him back from.

Wendell's number, 26, was in the second tier, with a driveway dropping steeply from the road to a turnaround in front of a garage set to the rear of the property. If the occupants didn't survive an avalanche, I supposed, their vehicles would.

With the houses so positioned that neighbors had only a rear view of each other, the architect had been able to indulge his fantasies, which apparently lay in the Peeping Tom department. The entire face of each house seemed to be of glass. I had to move to the very forward edge of the property and peer around the side of the house to see that, aside from a foot of concrete at its base, the whole facade was glass.

I returned to the house's entryway to press a large round button beside the door, hearing chimes echo through the interior. I waited, then rang it twice more at polite intervals, to no response. The garage on the other side of the driveway was closed, with no windows, so I couldn't tell whether a car was gone, even if I'd known how many he had. But the place seemed deserted.

I went to inspect the front again. Judged inaccessible no doubt, there were no drapes at all, offering an unobstructed view of the interior. It was an offer I couldn't refuse.

I inspected the soles of my tennies: not great traction. I took them off. When you've been used to gripping bars and rings and balance beams with your bare feet, you tend to put more stock in your toes than in your shoes.

The lip between the structure and the terrace's edge wasn't more than a foot, but I'd performed on less, so I ventured out to observe the interior of Windy Holman's home.

The clay of the bank, at least, felt firm, thanks to several days without rain, so I edged out, touching the glass for that illusion of balance a touchstone gives. About a third of the way out, my left foot touched a root, which provided an anchoring edge, and I spread my arms, sticking to the glass like one of those rubber Garfield figures you see peering through the back windows of cars.

The place was cavernous. Second-floor rooms lined a balcony, all three doors closed. The whole downstairs, however, was open—a "great room," in current design parlance—with kitchen, living, and dining rooms all merged in a continuous flow of black and white: white walls and black furniture, liberally edged with chrome.

Yet the house was not devoid of color. Like the backdrop of his post at the station, the walls of Windy's home were covered with fanned displays of T-shirts, hundreds of them, going back most likely to the beginning of his meteorologic career. Nailed together at the bottom, the T-shirts fanned out at the top, their lettering peeping out between the folds—NOR, BLA, JUN, RY, GH . . . Over every stretch of wall surface large enough to hold at least a few elementary-size shirts, the fans were like little sprays of fireworks, caught at midburst.

They were quite mesmerizing, actually, the colors carrying the eye in little hops from fan to fan and the mind into the tantalizing game of trying to figure out the words from the few visible letters.

I don't know how long I stood before remembering that my view was not exactly from the comfort of a lawn chair, and I turned to head back, in the process glancing down to the road below, where a bright red pickup stood in the turnout across from the development's gate.

Merde. My heart did a flip, nearly blowing my precarious balance, and I scuttled back to terra firma in a hurry. Clearly, this guy was better at tailing me than I was at tailing him. Why did I keep underestimating this man? The pretty-face syndrome, male version?

I reviewed my options and found them limited. There was only one entrance/exit to the development, a single untended gate at the bottom of the spiral of Skyline Drive. Obviously he knew that, since he was waiting right at its mouth.

The only tactic I could think of was to find a neighbor and beg the use of a phone. Whom I'd call I had yet to figure out. But I collected my shoes and socks and piled back in the Civic, urging it up the steep driveway, though it complained all the way.

I continued upward along the spiral, going over it in my mind. I could probably call the cops and get intervention, but that would mean going down to the station, filing charges, and eventually getting Gray involved. Neither my inclinations nor my plans for the day had any room for that. What I had on Harley at this point was small potatoes compared to the ultimate object of my quest: the link connecting my case to the Crucifixer killings. Harley's presence below escalated his candidacy for that link, but I was far from proving it. And putting a man in jail, only to have him make a U-turn and get out on bail, is akin to swatting at hornets: You just make them mad and more determined to come after you.

It was now twenty past one in the afternoon. My intended visit to the KEM station would mean backtracking half a mile and heading up Ridge Road, which would quickly put me into sparsely settled hills—a great place for a forced encounter.

"Plan B," I said aloud to myself. There must always be a Plan B. If I could lure him away somehow, I would forgo the station visit and drop down to the waterfront to head south, back to the island ferry.

I drove until I neared the top of the terraces, where the driveways wound down to the road, only a little less steeply, from the houses above. There, near the bottom of her drive, knelt a small gray-haired lady in a wide-brimmed straw gardening hat tied with a yellow polka-dotted scarf under her chin. She was kneeling on one of those green plastic gardening pads, having moved apparently down the curve of her drive from the house, snipping off the leaves of her spent spring bulbs. Since she was almost through, I didn't have the heart to tell her that her bulbs still needed those leaves as nourishment, and by tidily removing them she was weakening their chances of blooming next spring.

Instead, I showed her my P.I. license and asked whether I could use her phone to call the police.

She looked as alarmed as if I'd told her about the leaves, and I had to heartily reassure her that it was only a minor matter, I just needed to trade my car for one of theirs for a time, letting my voice and gestures trail off when it came to the reasons for the trade.

Finally, she stood with my help and led me up the drive and through a side door to her kitchen, where a yellow phone hung on the wall beside a corkboard full of cryptic notes. Then she withdrew for my privacy, but only just beyond the screen door, bent a little forward, peering through the screen. She still had not spoken, and I began to wonder if she were mute.

While the phone rang at the Emerald station, I did a bit of praying that Officer Weeks would be there and I would catch her in an uncharacteristic good mood.

She was in, Betty said, and put me through.

"Weeks," said the businesslike voice that answered. Ramona Weeks was always businesslike, which did not bode well for my request.

"It's Molly, Ramona," I said. I skipped the pleasantries, trying to impress her that I was every bit as businesslike as she. "I'm in a tight spot with the case I'm on, and I need some backup."

"What is transpiring?"

Ramona was the type of officer who'd arrived at

detective work by way of a degree in Criminology, rather than the more common route of the street beat. *Transpiring* was a short word, syllable-wise, in her lexicon.

"I've got somebody tailing me because I can already put him away on a charge of dumping toxic waste. But there's a good likelihood I can nail him on a more serious charge if I can just get him off my rear so I can finish my investigation. I was hoping you could help me out."

I didn't mention that the "more serious charge" might be murder; I was sure she'd just shift into high gear and arrest him on the spot.

"What exactly do you want of me?" Ramona said cautiously.

"Just switch cars with me. I'm in the Cranberry Cliffs development. If you could just drive a squad car up here and switch with me, we could probably get him to follow you instead. And by the time he saw it wasn't me, I'd be gone."

"Gone?"

"To check out the rest of my information," I said vaguely.

"A squad car?" There was disdain in her tone, as though I'd asked her to come by horse and buggy.

"Yeah, I think that'd be safest." Criminals don't usually chase after squad cars. "It would probably help if you came in uniform—at least the cap and jacket. Then I could put them on when I leave in the squad car. That should keep him from catching on for a while, till I can get clear of him." I held my breath for the answer. Had I pushed too far?

"Whatever," Ramona said sourly. "It might take me some time though. I don't know what-all requisitions need to be signed for such things."

"Yeah, okay, just as fast as you can, thanks." I gave her directions on reaching me and hung up.

When I came out through the screen door, my hostess broke her silence. "It sounds really quite dangerous," she said, making no secret of having listened to the conversation.

"Oh, not really, just a change of cars. It's routine." Whatever that meant. "Thanks very much for the use of your phone."

"Would you like something while you're waiting? I have some iced tea in the fridge. Or lemonade?"

"No, really," I said. "I'll just wait in my car. Thanks anyway. It shouldn't be long."

Actually, I'd have loved something cold and soothing to drink. But I didn't want to involve the poor lady any more than I already had. It could indeed become "quite dangerous."

With that in mind, I moved the car out of sight of the house and positioned it so I had a clear view of any vehicle coming up the drive, before I settled back to wait for Ramona.

Quickly impatient with idleness, I decided to go over my notes. When in doubt, do paperwork.

I hauled the accordion file off the floor of the passenger side and sorted out its contents. Though the earliest notes dated from little more than a week ago, it seemed as though I'd been on the case for months. And the stakes had been steadily rising.

I pulled Harley's file from the *Suspects* pocket and withdrew the receipts I'd found in his files—out-of-town expenditures on gas, food, etc. From the absence of lodging receipts, I gathered the drivers had slept in their trucks.

I'd intended to cross-check the receipts against the dates of the Crucifixer killings to see whether any would indicate that Harley had been out of town on one or more of those occasions, but since everything seemed to have been paid for in cash, there were no signatures to indicate who had used the services. One trip did seem to overlap with a Seattle killing, but that alone meant next to nothing if there were as many as three other drivers, such as I'd seen the day before.

So I turned again to the packet I'd found under Shirleen's bed and drew out the birth certificates, setting them side by side before me on the steering wheel.

In close proximity like that, something struck me about the documents that I hadn't noticed before. Alice's birth certificate from Utah had a pink background—not pink paper, but a faint wash of background color like that on the vehicle-registration certificates, though here they were bunnies with bows on their ears instead of Washington's head on a chain of coins. Mary Alice's birth certificate, on the other hand, was a flat black-and-white.

I examined it more closely. The paper was thinner, smoother than the other, and when I held it up to the light I detected the faintest of prints in the background—smiling cherubs, though they, too, were colorless.

A copy? Not in itself significant, I supposed. Birth certificates get lost and are replaced with photocopies if needed for school registration, applying for social-security cards, whatever. But squinting at each segment of the information in turn, the style of the letters and numbers was uniformly ornate, with little flourishes on the final stroke. But in three areas the style faltered, as though traced. Or forged.

I held the document up to the light and could see that the faint background bleed-through was blanked out in those areas, as though someone had whited them out and drawn something else over them.

I pulled my Washington State map out of the door pocket and looked up Tyrone, the town in which the Gabriel Clinic was located. About an hour and a half northeast. By the time Ramona arrived I had changed my itinerary.

CHAPTER 25

As Ramona pulled up I could see she was wearing the uniform—at least from the waist up. That would probably cost me double.

"Wow, thanks, Ramona," I said as she opened the door. "I owe you big-time."

"You certainly do." She wasn't smiling, and the body language of her entire long lithe figure was saying, *Let's get this over with as quickly as possible.*

"I'll give you the file on this guy when I've seen how he fits into my case. Besides the environmental charge, there's probably forgery, tax evasion—who knows what-all."

"Gee, thanks." She did not sound impressed.

"Did you see him? The red pickup?"

"Across the street, facing the view. Very subtle."

"If you can get him to follow you, I'm going to head north. I'll check with you later, see what happened."

"And return the car."

"And return the car."

"What's this bozo's name?"

"Well, take your pick. There's Harley Abbott, or

Roman Marcello, or Julius D'Amato, Anthony Amoroso—"

"I get the idea."

"Hope you're not swayed by a pretty face and a perfect bod. He's got 'em and he flaunts 'em. But unless you're into S and M, you might want to pass."

"Charming."

She passed over the jacket and cap. Both could accommodate two of me, but I figured I could shed them once I was sure he'd taken the bait. It took both of us to move back the seat in my Civic to make room for her longer legs, and an even greater effort to move up the seat in the squad car, but then we were ready to roll.

She left first, agreeing to park my car in the station's lot and leave the keys with Gray. I couldn't see the road from the third terrace and really wanted to watch, to see if he fell for it, but I didn't want to risk blowing it now that I'd indebted myself to Ramona for life, so I stayed put.

I gave it five minutes before I cruised slowly down the spiral. No red pickup in sight. But I knew I'd have to keep my eye on the rearview mirror: Whatever else he was, Harley was no fool. I knew I had to consider him a potentially dangerous, if not deadly, adversary. But then, who was there on my list of suspects who was not? What was it Mary Alice had said that first day in my office?

Who knows what she might be capable of? What anybody might? I was still in no position to narrow the field. Suspiciousness is an occupational hazard—my least favorite, next to violence.

The town of Tyrone, Washington, proved to be little more than a few deep breaths border to border. The biggest thing in it was the Gabriel Clinic, an elaborate affair of stone and stucco that must have taken big bucks to build, finished off with fat white columns holding up the portico. My guess was that this was where the rich came to have their indiscretions or their vanities attended to with maximum anonymity. Even the name was not prominently displayed, only white on white around the rim of the portico.

That sense was reinforced when I noticed two well-dressed, very pregnant young girls walking along a path that circled a stately gray Victorian on the hill just beyond the clinic. I decided to leave the squad car—and the uniform—on the street.

The heavy teak door was locked, with a little square onyx box to the side instructing the caller to press it and wait for instructions. Above, I noticed a camera trained on my position and wished I'd kept the police gear on, for added credibility. On the other hand, they might ask to see my badge, so I guessed I was stuck with my own identity. I fished my P.I. license out of my bag and held it up for the camera when asked to identify myself. I was there to pick up some records for my client, I said. Close enough to the truth, and it got me in.

Beyond the doors was a young woman at a polished teak table, painting her nails to the exact color of her coral bracelet. She barely glanced up as I approached.

I repeated my name and proffered my license. "Miss Abbott has reason to believe that her copy of her birth certificate has been tampered with and asked me to come for a copy of the original. It has to do with the inheritance of a substantial estate," I added, suspecting that this was a place where money spoke.

"Records," the young woman replied, barely

glancing up from her task. "Down the hall, then right, then left, first door on the right."

I set off down the hall, muttering the directions like a mantra. Right then left, door on right? Or left then right . . . ?

The only branch from the main hall was to the right, so I turned down it. At the end was another, branching both left and right. "Right then left," she'd said. I was almost positive. (Directions are not really an area where I shine. There always seem to be so many other choices.)

I turned left, found a door on each side of the hall, neither marked as to its function. I tried the door to the right. Locked. I tried the one to the left, which opened to a small room with a single desk and its occupant, a middle-aged woman who looked up and smiled at me, a little surprised as though she didn't get many visitors. The nameplate on the desk read MARCELLA CHISUM.

I told her what my business was, and she looked at my license with a lively interest. "A private investigator? Really? I didn't think that sort of thing actually existed. At least not anymore. Not since Sam Spade and Nick and Nora Charles and those people."

I assured her that I did exist and handed her the copy of the birth certificate.

"That's one of ours all right," she said, "before we were on computer. I can check the files if you like."

She kept talking as she crossed to her left and opened a door, flicking on the light in a smaller room with almond metal files running its length. "They call these the inactive files in here. The active ones are across the hall on computer, everything for the past twenty-four years. Before that, there's just the paper. In here. Hardly anybody ever comes for one of these."

My breath caught. Had I stumbled onto pay dirt?

She puttered about in the narrow room, opening one drawer and then another, muttering to herself softly as people do who are used to being alone. "Mary Alice Abbott. Shirleen Abbott . . ."

"If you can't find it under Abbott, you might try Holman," I called to her. "The mother's maiden name." I spelled it for her.

She puttered some more, then moved to the far end of the room where I couldn't see her, and there were the scrapes of drawers opening and closing, then a smaller metallic tap, and the scrape of another drawer.

She came back holding a manila folder, but with a small frown on her pleasant face. "I don't know if this is what you want," she said, peering through bifocals at the white sheet inside. "It's Holman, but it's only Mary, not Mary Alice, and there's an Alice, but no Shirleen."

Already my hand was reaching for the folder, but she picked the paper out and studied it some more. "I wouldn't even have looked there, in the closed files, except that Louise Apple, who had this job before me, made a cross-file, on index cards." She looked up with an apologetic expression. "We don't have all that much to do."

I don't think I breathed throughout her entire monologue. I tried to look over her shoulder, but she began moving toward the rear of the room. "Louise had made this reference under *Holman, Shirleen*, then *See Alice. Mary*. It was filed in the A's, under Alice."

I briefly considered snatching the document from her hand and running like hell. "Could I just take a look?" I asked, my voice coming out with a croak as I followed her with outstretched arm.

"Better yet, I'm making you a copy," she said, arriving at the small photocopier. "Then if it's not the right one . . ." She made an expansive gesture.

It seemed to take forever for the copier to warm up, the orange command to WAIT feeling like an intentional tease. When it finally turned green, the woman fitted the paper to the guidelines as precisely as though the result would forever bear her name.

Then at last she poked the green button, the gears whirred, and a paper finally slid into the tray on the left. She plucked it out and handed it to me, still warm.

"Is there a charge?" I asked in barely a whisper.

"Oh, my goodness, no," she said. "Isn't that what we're here for, to provide records?"

I reached out the hand that wasn't clutching the paper and grasped hers. "Thank you, Marcella Chisum," I said. "Thank you very much."

Then I made my getaway swiftly down one hall and then the next, as though someone might step through a door at any time to stop me. And I didn't slow my pace until I had made it to the squad car.

I was almost afraid to look. Then I almost could not believe what I saw. *Name of baby:* Mary Holman. *Mother:* Alice Holman. *Date of birth:* three years earlier than the August birth date on the altered copy. *Father:* Wendell Holman.

Which meant . . . ?

With only a small fraction of my mind allotted to the task, I drove to a fast-food place and used the phone while I waited for my grilled chicken sandwich.

"Hi. It's me."

"I'm glad you called," Simon said heartily. "I've heard from my colleague in Utah. He thinks he's found your nanny."

"Oh. Good." Could my brain absorb more?

"One Nola Tuttle. She was listed as the person to

be notified on the hospital records where Shirleen gave birth to Alice. And apparently she's still alive. My contact went to the address given, and to all appearances, she's still there; there's mail in the box for her. The neighbors said she left suddenly last week."

"Wow."

"Have you had a chance to look into the cause of death of the parents?"

I groaned. "I'm not even close to that number on my list."

"If you would permit me then," Simon said, "I found myself with time on my hands this morning and wondered if their deaths had made the Olympia papers. As pillars of the island community, presumably."

"And?"

"They had. A rather nasty business, I'm afraid. She shot him. And then herself."

"Whoa!" My mind went blank. "Motive?" I asked.

"It seems that his daughter's baby was his."

"Jesus," I whispered. No wonder the father's name was listed as unknown.

"Apparently the children dropped out of sight, presumably with the nanny in Utah, until the whole thing blew over and they could come back to the family home."

"Or what was left of the family," I said. "It seems there are a lot of nameless fathers in this case." I told Simon about my findings at the clinic.

"Quite a family tree," he said. "Where are you headed now?"

"To the ferry, I guess. I made a four o'clock appointment at Mary Alice's to see if I could corner Shirleen and get some answers out of her. Now I've got more questions than I knew I had."

"What about the husband?"

"Oh, he's a bad boy all right. But how he fits in the genealogy, let alone the murders? I haven't a clue."

"You need any backup?"

"I think I'm okay. I just need to absorb some of this stuff. Thanks for your help, Simon, I'll be in touch."

I picked up my grilled chicken and sat in the squad car munching without tasting. Then I fired up the motor and headed south again.

It was lucky I had the police car, because I was a good twenty miles per hour over the speed limit on the secondary roads before I hit I-5 and floored it. I couldn't have said exactly why I was in such a hurry, but I felt an urgency deep in my gut. And it only intensified when I reached the top of Wendell's driveway and saw the garage standing open and empty.

I left the squad car at the top, motor running, and went down to check the house.

It looked unchanged; only the mailbox by the driveway stood open, its flap down. The box was empty, but there was a scrap of something near the post, and I bent to pick it up.

It seemed to be a torn strip from a photograph, fuzzy, as though shot from a distance or through glass. The print had been torn diagonally, the left corner curled as though twisted, the glossy surface peeled at the top edge from the coarser paper backing. Only a ragged couple of inches wide, the strip was still recognizable as the curve of a breast and a bare arm stretched to a glint of metal handcuff.

CHAPTER 26

I BARELY MADE THE FERRY. Though I'd turned on the two-way radio as I approached Emerald from the north, I turned it off when I got back in the car at Wendell's. I didn't want to take the time to switch cars, so didn't want to hear any calls for the return of this one.

After three atypical days of March sunshine, the clouds had begun gathering that morning, and by now the sky was darkening rapidly, like the accelerated frames of a film depicting nightfall. Once I'd cleared Emerald I turned on the siren the rest of the way to Port Condor; it was nearly five, and I wanted to get on before the after-work line began forming for the ferry.

When I crested the hill and saw the bay below, I could see that a substantial line had already formed—commuters trying to get home, perhaps, before the storm.

I shrugged on the officer's jacket and set the cap on my head to drive past the line, straight up to where the yellow-slickered crew was just finishing a loading. I turned the siren off only when one had come up to my window.

"Police emergency," I said in my most authoritative manner.

The woman peered at me a moment, then nodded and gestured me on, calling to her comrade to let me pass.

I had stopped the squad car where directed, in the second-to-last row on, when I glanced in the rearview mirror to see a bright red pickup in the lot, its driver talking to the same woman who had let me on. Then the last row of vehicles—none of them red pickups—filled in behind, blocking my view.

The ferry started up soon after, and I got out, feeling claustrophobic in the pack of metal, needing some good salt air. I made my way up the once-white metal stairs, past the lines at the food concessions, and out through a side door, bucking the wind to stand against the rail at the stern, watching the receding coast of the mainland, my mind busy with all that had gone on there.

The ferry's motor, driving the wheels that churned the water, was so loud, I heard nothing until a round hard object dug into my back and a voice said, "We meet again."

I didn't need to turn to know who it was, but I did anyway—slowly, with my hands open to show the regrettable fact that I was unarmed. I virtually never carry a gun, only when I know I'm heading into certain danger, and when I'd left the island three days ago I'd had no idea that my case would prove so intimately linked to the Crucifixer killings—among other extralegal activities.

"Well, how lovely to see you again," I said, studying Harley's face for signs that he was capable of point-blank killing. I could see that he was.

"You've been poking your nose in my business again," he said from a tight throat. "And I told you you wouldn't like me when I'm angry."

"I don't much like you anyway," I said. I was standing with my back touching the rail, which hit me just above the shoulder blades. I calculated how high I'd have to spring to wrap my arms around it backward. Harley was standing about five feet from me. Too far. I'd have to coax him closer.

I leaned back against the rail, raising my arms so that my elbows rested on top, in what would have been a suggestive pose if I'd had more to suggest with. "I thought you'd be used to women following you around," I said.

He didn't look as if he was falling for it, but his features did relax some; this was familiar territory for him. "Not when I'm working," he said, a little less harshly. He took a step closer then, extending the gun as though to caress my torso with it, and I figured that was going to be as good as it would get.

I jumped up and back, hooking my arms over the rail and kicking out with my legs, the right aimed at his face, the left at his gun.

Both connected, and he rocked backward, the gun skittering off along the slippery deck.

I leapt for it while he was still recovering his balance and got there first, grabbing it in both hands from a crouch. "Now," I said as I slowly rose, gun leveled, "let's have a little chat on my terms. Tell me about the Crucifixer."

I was hoping to catch him off-guard, so I could tell something from his reaction, but he only said peevishly, "What the hell would I know about that?"

"Don't be coy," I said, backing off to an unreachable distance. "I know more than you think." Whatever that meant.

"You must," he said, scowling, "because I don't know what you're talking about."

"Don't you?" I said. "That's how your stepdaughter was killed."

"So? What does that have to do with me?"

It was a remark just candidly selfish enough to believe. This was a man driven only by ego and vanity. He could kill, but probably only if it served his immediate interests rather than the compulsions of his psyche.

"Who else would have reason to kill her?"

"How would I know? I haven't seen her in twenty years."

"Did she leave the household before or after you left?"

"I dunno," he said, his eyes on the gun. "She ran off a lot while I was there, be gone a couple of days. Then when I left, she came asking to stay with me."

"Why with you?"

"Why not? I guess she felt comfortable with me." He tried a weak imitation of his cocky smile. "And great sex, of course."

"Why did you leave?"

Harley had been edging toward the rail, and I let him, keeping the same amount of distance between us. He leaned an elbow on the rail now, apparently finding it a more casual, face-saving position.

"I was never meant to be domesticated," he said.

"But you and Shirleen have kept seeing each other."

He raised an eyebrow but did not ask how I knew. "Not at first. She was steamed, threatened me with everything she could think of."

"Like what?"

"She'd bankrolled my business, took me out from under the cars and into the driver's seat."

"Generous."

"It had its price."

"So you lost that when you left?"

"By then I knew I could make it without her money. I'd made some connections in Seattle."

"And she followed you?"

"Not for a while. I'd given her a phony address. I owed her money and didn't want her coming after me."

"But she found you?"

"Alice found me first. She was all strung out. She and her mother fought like alley cats."

"Why didn't she run to her uncle if she needed protection?"

"It was just as bad with him. He was always calling her a harlot, saying she led men into temptation."

"What did he mean by that?"

"Who knows? That was the way both of them talked."

"Both Wendell and Shirleen?"

"Yeah. All that hellfire-and-brimstone stuff."

"*Was* Alice seductive toward him?"

"She tried to stay away from him mostly. But he was on her all the time."

"Did Shirleen know?"

"I doubt it. He was a shifty one, and she'd probably have hit the roof. She liked her men devoted only to her."

"Her men? So Shirleen's relationship with Wendell also was sexual?"

He shrugged. "Had been, I guess."

"Was he around a lot?"

"At first. But he couldn't seem to handle it after the marriage. I didn't see him for a while, then he was back again right before I left. The two of them had a real screaming match, him yelling how she'd seduced him as a kid. I split. I didn't need that kind of hassle. I'd gotten bored with her anyway: too stuck on herself."

"Did Alice ever talk to you about the situation there? About her relationship to her mother, or her uncle?"

"She didn't talk much, Alice." The cocky grin again. "You could say she was more action-oriented."

"Was your relationship with her sexual while you were living there?"

He grinned. "She was a tease, what can I say?"

"And after you left? When was that?"

"I couldn't take more than a year of it. Then Alice came around when she ran off. And I'm a friendly kind of guy."

The sky had been getting steadily blacker, the wind whipping the waves into a frenzy. We could barely hear each other with raised voices. Thunder had been rumbling in the distance, the streaks of lightning like strokes from a silver pen against the dark sky. Now there was a sharp slap of thunder so close, both of us jumped a little, and I glanced back to see the lights on Prince Island go out.

The ferry was nearing Port Angel, and I tried to decide what to do with Harley. I was way late for my scheduled meeting at the house and didn't want to stop for paperwork with whatever authorities, so I guessed I was stuck with him for the time being. I directed him to walk ahead of me along the outer rim of the ship. Our position was not visible from the inside shelter, and no one else had been foolish enough to come out under that threatening sky. I knew the ferry well enough to avoid most of the traffic getting back to their cars, and started Harley off in that direction.

"How long do you think you can keep that thing on me?" he said as we moved toward the stairs.

"Long enough."

I stayed close behind the man so the gun wouldn't be too visible. But after all, I'd been seen driving a squad car and wearing a cop cap, so who would question my having a prisoner at gunpoint?

"Get in," I said when we reached the car. "You're driving."

"I usually am."

"I'm sure. I caught part of your act at the Blue Moon Motel."

"Did you?" he said, sounding pleased, as I slid into the backseat behind him. "How did you like it?"

"They'll probably love it at Leavenworth. Though the positions may be reversed."

"You've got nothing on me, you know," he said, starting the motor with the key I tossed him.

"That's for the courts to decide," I said, my mind busy elsewhere. I could see rain beginning to pelt the first cars off the ferry—heavy drops, as though the sky had held its breath as long as it could and was now letting it all out at once. I could see no lights on in Port Angel.

"Turn on the police band," I told Harley. "I want to see if the power's out all over the island."

There was nothing but static until we cleared the overhang of the ferry, then several voices seemed to be talking at once. I couldn't make out much of what they were saying and wanted Harley to keep both hands on the wheel, so I had no real clue to what was going on until I heard a voice say "Glass Avenue," then another that said "standoff."

A series of images flashed across my mind's eye, and I didn't like any of them. "Step on it," I told Harley, though we were already going faster than Wolf Road could safely accommodate.

As we sped toward Grace, the story was barely sketched in between episodes of static, while thunder followed lightning through the relentless rain.

". . . says he'll kill all of them first," I heard, then words like *unstable* and *Seattle swat team*. I worried about Mary Alice: Was she among the apparent hostages, or only a wretched bystander as her world came crashing down?

Because of the squad car we were able to drive a good deal closer to the scene than we might have otherwise. When we were finally stopped, a young officer unknown to me peered down at the window. I lowered mine, identified myself and my client, and showed him my license. "That's her beside Chief Belgium," I said, craning my neck out the window. "I need to get to her. Could you hold this suspect while I see what I can do here?"

I didn't give him much chance to say no, climbing out of the car and turning the gun over to him. "It's his," I said. "There are a whole string of charges to hold him on. I'll fill the Chief in as soon as this is over."

I made my way through the layers of bystanders, reporters, and law-enforcement personnel, in that order, toward the tall diamond-paned living room windows, behind which a single candle burned, set on the floor before the figures of Wendell and Shirleen Holman.

Shirleen looked as though she'd been weeping for hours, her mascara in little stripes down the front of her face, her hair nearly as disheveled as mine. If she survived this, I thought, she was going to hate the pictures of herself in the papers.

The lightning, with the rain, had mostly passed, and the flashbulbs of the news photographers were now the brightest lights, bursts of brilliance that made their aftermath seem even darker in the dusk that had come early with the storm. Inside, the votive candle, stuck in an ornate glass holder, had burned low, the flame leaping wildly from within the hollowed wax, sending the shadows of the two figures lurching against the surfaces behind.

It was only as I drew closer to the police barricade that I spotted another figure in the room, seated before the cold hearth in a wing chair so tall its back nearly swallowed the frail form. I stared at the figure, feeling the back of my own head reverberate in memory. The nanny, I thought; it had to be. Maybe she was just too mean to die.

I pushed on toward Mary Alice, elbowing hips as I went. The Chief raised the bullhorn he held and bellowed into it, the hoarseness of his voice suggesting he'd been doing this awhile. "Come on, Mister Holman, you know there's no way out, and you don't want to kill any more people, so just put down the gun and let the women leave."

By way of response Wendell gesticulated with his free hand, pointing at the nanny, then at Shirleen. I could see Mary Alice's agonized profile, and I pushed on toward her and touched her arm.

She swung around with alarm, then seeing who it was, enveloped me in a tight embrace.

When she released me, her look was equally intense. "He's threatening to shoot all of them, himself too," she said.

"Have you spoken to him?"

"I've tried, but he just keeps shaking his head and saying that I'll be better off."

"The old woman was their nanny?"

"I guess so. I don't know why she's here; I thought she'd died years ago. They were all there, like that, when I got home for our meeting. The door was locked and he wouldn't let me in."

I looked around for a spot of privacy, decided the only possibility was inside the Grace patrol car behind us. I took her elbow, guided her into its backseat, and pulled the door shut behind us.

I'd seldom felt so awkward. How do you tell a person this sort of thing? Especially under these circumstances. "Mary Alice," I began, "I've just been to the clinic where you were born, to see what I could find in your records there. I think I need to tell you what I learned."

She looked at me steadily. "Uncle Wendell is my father," she said, in a voice still as the eye of a storm. "Isn't he?"

"You've known that?"

"In a way, I think. I've thought of him as my father for so long, it just feels like it couldn't be any other way."

"Have you told him that?"

She regarded me. "No," she said slowly, her eyes losing focus then, looking inward. Until all at once she got out of the squad car on the other side and approached Chief Belgium, who handed over the bullhorn.

"Uncle Wendell," she called, her voice startlingly strong, not all of which seemed due to the magnification powers of the bullhorn.

His head swung sharply toward her, as though he had noticed it too.

"Please, if you love me," she said, "don't take my parents from me."

His face stared through the glass, though I wasn't sure if he could see her.

"Do you remember how it felt? Both your parents gone, suddenly alone in the world? Please don't do that to me. I love you. You've been everything to me I could ask of a father. Don't leave me."

Then Shirleen took advantage of his distraction and lunged for the gun. He jerked it away, and his mouth twisted, shouting at her over and over, "Seducer! Whore! You make everything dirty!"

Another flashbulb popped, briefly illuminating the room beyond the candle's light, and my gaze was drawn to that stairless balcony at the far end, resting on the five beams that crossed the room lengthwise beneath its lofty cathedral ceiling.

I moved to Mary Alice's side and spoke in her ear. Her answer was enough to go on. I spoke to Chief Belgium, too, but didn't wait around to hear his objections.

I struggled through the crowd toward the far end of the house, wondering if I couldn't find a more sparsely populated island to set out my shingle on next time.

I passed through the covered walkway between the garage and the house, then around to the side, looking up at the dark windows of Shirleen's bedroom, over the windowless end wall of the living room. They seemed to take up little more than half the depth of the house, strengthening my hunch that the layout of the upstairs rear might be a mirror image of its front.

Which was more than I could say for the landscaping. Once out of sight of the street, the grooming of the trees and shrubs was shoddy, the flower beds without bloom. But there was no mistaking the tree Mary Alice had said led to Alice's old room—an ancient oak as gnarled and twisted as Nola Tuttle. I wasted no time in mounting it, shedding my shoes and socks and jumping for the first branch.

The wet bark was slippery with rain and redolent of sap, the new leaves releasing little sprays of water as I passed, as gentle as a baptismal font. I found myself reveling in the climb, whatever violations of the laws of Nature had prompted it. From my vantage point I could almost forget what was going on inside that house.

Until Mary Alice's voice on the bullhorn filtered back. "Whatever else you've done, you've never hurt me."

And another bit of the arithmetic fell into place. Except for Alice, all the victims of the Crucifixer had been young women about Mary Alice's present age. Substitutes to appease what drove him, to spare the one person he genuinely loved, while all other women were considered evil?

But was that possible, I wondered, for such a driven person to exercise even that much discrimination and restraint? Alice had protected Mary Alice when she herself was being molested, but what had protected her since? I couldn't see Shirleen in the role. But Mary Alice's trust of her uncle/father was unarguable and could never have been earned by an adult who had crossed the sexual boundaries.

I was climbing the last few feet to the windowsill, thinking how Wendell must have climbed this tree to reach Alice's bedroom all those years before, when suddenly an image hit me with the force of an electric current, as though the storm's lightning had returned to strike down this very tree: climbing at night to a girl's bedroom window. Strangling her with her own stripped nightgown.

And another image loomed, of a fan of purple T-shirts nailed to a white wall: GE, GEN, NE, EE, SEE . . .

Wendell, the Romeo Strangler? It would have been about the time of Shirleen's marriage, the victims roughly the same age she must have been when she'd seduced him, as he'd apparently seen it. And it hadn't even started there. Father to daughter, daughter to brother, brother to sister . . . like a contagious disease.

I reached for the stout branch above to steady myself, but it gave way, flopping like a broken arm from an old wound. Wendell's limp. Had that been what it took to end his climbs?

With a major effort that made my injured right-shoulder muscle feel like it was being ripped apart, I pulled myself up to the deep windowsill.

It took a moment to regain my balance before I could examine the window. I'd been afraid it would be locked, even boarded over; but apparently the removal of the girls and the sealing off of that wing had seemed prevention enough. After a few bangs along the frame on all four sides, the window was raisable, and I boosted myself over the edge of the sill and dropped to the floor below.

I fumbled for a light switch and found a knob on a standing lamp. The musty, dark-red carpeting was hardly a feminine pastel usually chosen for daughters, and the posters on the walls were equally heavy. The largest, of the rock group Black Sabbath, stood watch over the bed, with its stiff figures and hollow stares. It was in bleak black and white; the only spot of color I had to peer closer to discern. It was red-dyed hair, topping the stony face of the young Alice in her last school picture before being taken out to hide her pregnancy. Glued among the other faces, it looked right at home.

There was nothing in the room to suggest that a childhood had ever passed there.

But there was no time for reflection. I moved quickly to the door and opened it onto the hallway layout I'd expected.

I turned right, feeling my way to the corridor's end, then left. Ahead was the door Mary Alice had said would be there, opening onto that stairless balcony.

There was no lock on the door when I reached it, but neither did it open, the smooth knob twisting in my hand too loosely to engage the mechanism behind it.

The voices rose from below all too clearly: "You're as guilty as I am!" Wendell was shouting. "You stole my innocence, my youth!"

"You compare that to what you've done?!"

"You knew perfectly well what I was doing, and you did nothing to stop it."

"But Alice! Your own sister, for heaven's sake. The mother of your child."

"You're the one who told me to get rid of her."

"I only said to get her out of town. So she wouldn't ruin all the good work I've done on her daughter. Mary Alice is without sin, entirely without sin, thanks to my upbringing."

"Mary Alice is pure because she has none of you in her. She's the only truly good person to come out of this family since Mother, God rest her soul."

"Mother!" Shirleen said contemptuously. "Do I have to remind you that our *mother* killed our *father*? Well, my father anyway; God knows who yours was, you bastard!"

"Don't call me that! I've told you never to call me that!"

I remembered the absence of joy in the father's

expression in that first photograph that had included Wendell. I twisted the knob again.

"She would have poisoned Mary Alice's mind against me," Wendell was saying. "I couldn't bear that. Mary Alice respects me, looks up to me."

"But to *kill* her, your own flesh and blood, just like all those other wretched girls. It's barbaric!"

Then the old woman's voice sliced through, shriller still. "He couldn't even do it. Couldn't drive the stake, couldn't light the match. Miserable excuse for a man."

Through the din, I thought any noise I might make would go unheard, so I banged on the knob with my fist, wrenching right, then left, and suddenly the thing engaged, releasing the door with a kind of startled *thunk*. The increase in the volume from below was not a welcome consequence.

"That girl should have died the day she was born," the old woman was screeching. "She was conceived in sin, the worst kind of sin. But in the end, it was me had to do the Lord's work."

I stuck my head out. Below, Shirleen's body swung toward the old woman. "*You? You* killed Alice?!"

The nanny was on her feet beneath the oversize painting of the Madonna, her frail body bobbing in time to her shrill words. "She was doomed by your evil ways, missy. You with your short skirts and your see-through nighties and your pretty little face. You seduced your own father, crazed your poor mother. Then you started on your brother. Look at what you've reduced him to!"

Wendell swung the gun toward her, shouting, "Witch!" and fired, her form crumpling to the floor as though there had never been life in it at all.

Shirleen stared at the sight, then looked toward the

window, as though to see whether the shooting had been observed. I slipped inside, shutting the door and flattening myself against it.

I hadn't heard Mary Alice's voice in some time but spotted her now sitting on the fender of the patrol car on the far side of Chief Belgium, no bullhorn in hand. Her face was in shadow, her shoulders slumped. How much, I wondered, had she heard of this last exchange about her relatives, and how would it affect her?

A flashbulb burst, and the figure of Harley Abbott was illumined, lounging against another squad car, his handcuffed wrists resting against his groin.

Wendell saw him, too, and Shirleen saw the gun swing toward him.

"No!" she yelped. "Not him!"

"You with your infernal talk of virtue, still wallowing in sin with that hoodlum!" Wendell yelled.

"He's my husband!" Shirleen wailed. "The marriage was never annulled. Why don't you listen to me! In the eyes of the church he is still my husband, and our union is blessed. You and I, it was always a sin, and I've vowed to God never to weaken again."

Then the gun went off and Harley dropped, and I fast-forwarded to execute my part to try to salvage the wreckage of my client's family.

I raced to the end of the balcony and swung my legs over, my feet landing flat on the foremost beam, which crossed the room directly over the heads of the two of them, now wrestling for the gun.

"But I *love* him!" Shirleen was keening.

"What would you know about love?" Wendell roared.

And I took off, an easy run on a track twice the width of a four-inch balance beam. Unless you factored in the height. Ahead, brother and sister and revolver formed a twisting triumvirate, into whose vortex I leaped, landing on the mercifully well-padded Wendell, sending him and Shirleen sprawling and the gun sailing out of reach, as Chief Belgium and his troops burst through the door and gathered them up.

Over the next hour Wendell was taken off to the single cell of the Grace jail, Shirleen to its office to give her already self-sanitizing statement, and Harley to the hospital in Sweetbay for treatment of the flesh wound to his thigh.

Mary Alice refused to go into the house again, so I sat with her in the gazebo in a stand of pines while her tears flowed, the only words making it through the fierce statement, "I knew she couldn't be my mother."

Then, after Chief Belgium had retired his men and chased off the paparazzi, he approached, looking even more tired and uncomfortable than usual. He made brief eye contact and extended his hand to me, saying in his rough basso voice, "Thanks for your help tonight."

I gave him my best shot at a smile. "Anytime," I said, though I was fervently hoping it would not be anytime soon.

EPILOGUE

HARLEY SURVIVED THE SHOT TO HIS THIGH, though he won't be performing his whipping act anytime soon—at least not from that end of the whip. And both the I.R.S. and E.P.A. perked up at news of his exploits.

The memory of the fear in Mrs. Erchak's eyes kept me from calling the alien police, but I figured that route at least would dry up with Harley indisposed.

Shirleen is probably still insisting to anyone who will listen that she has no idea what her brother could have been ranting about; he must be insane.

And Wendell, Mary Alice tells me, is still on suicide watch in his Seattle jail cell, awaiting trial for the first three Crucifixer killings. She visits him twice a week, on the days she doesn't have therapy.

She left the family house for good that night and quit her job at the dry cleaner's the next day. She's decided, she told me when she had me over for dinner at her new apartment, to go back to school and study nursing. There's enough money in her own name, she says, left by her (great) grandparents, to last her for the rest of her life. But she wants to work. "I need to be with people. Other people," she said over the chocolate soufflé. "I want to really *do* something with my life, something that will make a difference."

She didn't add anything about making up for whatever her relatives might have done, but I suspect that was in there somewhere.

As for me, I called my parents the next morning, said yes, I'd love to come see them, caught a flight that afternoon. I'd never felt so lucky. For my lover, too, although I figured Gray could use the week to cool down from the news photos of my three-point landing on the Crucifixer.

Then I got back to business.

Match wits with the bestselling
MYSTERY WRITERS
in the business!

SARA PARETSKY
"Paretsky's name always makes the top of the list when people talk about the new female operatives." —*The New York Times Book Review*

☐ BLOOD SHOT	20420-8	$6.99
☐ BURN MARKS	20845-9	$6.99
☐ INDEMNITY ONLY	21069-0	$6.99
☐ GUARDIAN ANGEL	21399-1	$6.99
☐ KILLING ORDERS	21528-5	$6.99
☐ DEADLOCK	21332-0	$6.99
☐ TUNNEL VISION	21752-0	$6.99
☐ WINDY CITY BLUES	21873-X	$6.99
☐ A WOMAN'S EYE	21335-5	$6.99
☐ WOMEN ON THE CASE	22325-3	$6.99

HARLAN COBEN
Winner of the Edgar, the Anthony, and the Shamus Awards

☐ DEAL BREAKER	22044-0	$5.50
☐ DROP SHOT	22049-5	$5.50
☐ FADE AWAY	22268-0	$5.50
☐ BACK SPIN	22270-2	$5.50

RUTH RENDELL
"There is no finer mystery writer than Ruth Rendell." —*San Diego Union Tribune*

☐ THE CROCODILE BIND	21865-9	$5.99
☐ SIMISOLA	22202-8	$5.99
☐ KEYS TO THE STREET	22392-X	$5.99

LINDA BARNES

☐ COYOTE	21089-5	$5.99
☐ STEEL GUITAR	21268-5	$5.99
☐ BITTER FINISH	21606-0	$4.99
☐ SNAPSHOT	21220-0	$5.99
☐ CITIES OF THE DEAD	22095-5	$5.50
☐ DEAD HEAT	21862-4	$5.50
☐ HARDWARE	21223-5	$5.99

At your local bookstore or use this handy page for ordering:
DELL READERS SERVICE, DEPT. DIS
2451 South Wolf Road, Des Plaines, IL . 60018
Please send me the above title(s). I am enclosing $_____
(Please add $2.50 per order to cover shipping and handling.) Send check or money order—no cash or C.O.D.s please.

Dell

Ms./Mrs./Mr. _____

Address _____

City/State _____ Zip _____

DGM-12/97
Prices and availability subject to change without notice. Please allow four to six weeks for delivery.